THE FALCON RISES

By

M.L. Bullock

I dedicate this book to Carolann. You were an oasis of peace in a time of trouble, a sheltering rock for us all. We miss you every day. I love you.

Akhenaten's Poem to Nefertiti

The Hereditary Princess, Great of Favor,
Mistress of happiness,
Gay with the two feathers,
At hearing whose voice one rejoices,
Soothing the heart of the King at home,
Pleased at all that is said,
The great and beloved wife of the King,
Lady of the two lands, Neferneferuaten Nefertiti,
Living forever.

—Akhenaten, 1340 BC

Chapter One

The Bloody Throne—Queen Tiye

I tossed and turned on my golden couch, the sounds of the soothing fountain drowned out by the noise of silly little girls playing a hand-clapping game under my balcony. I huffed, slung back the silken sheets and waved the startled attendant away. There would be no sleep for me this afternoon, and I longed for sleep— just a moment's respite from the sadness that filled my soul. My husband, the great and splendid Amenhotep, languished in Thebes. And if I had any hope of navigating the future successfully, I must remain here in the Grand Harem away from my husband's court. It was difficult, but I was willing to sacrifice whatever time I had with Amenhotep in order to secure our dynasty.

I could not trust these things to men, not even my brother Huya or my husband's most trusted adviser, Ramose. Men were no match for the minds of powerful women, especially women like Kiya and her groping relatives.

I knew what the prophets of Amun had declared: "No child of Tiye's will ever take the throne. She is of common blood." Yet my husband loved me more than he ever feared them. And that love and devotion had cost us everything—it cost us our son, Thutmose. Beautiful, smiling Thutmose, cut down in the desert at the foot of the sphinx, supposedly by some jealous god of the Red Sands. But I knew better. My husband knew better too. It had been the wretched priests who slew my son and left him to die in the sand. His body had never been recovered, but I knew he was dead, his light stolen from this world. What was worse was Thutmose would not be reborn, would never rise from death. His body had not been prepared for the journey, and he would undoubtedly remain in the darkness for all eternity.

It had been a cruel deed and one I would never forget. Neither would Amenhotep. Just last night as I lay beside him, he whispered to me through his dry lips, "Do not forget Thutmose. Do not forget my son."

Obediently I had prevented the tears from falling. The order had been given: no tears would be shed in my presence, not even my own. I agreed and lovingly traced his face with my finger. I held him in my arms until he began to retch the black bile, and then I slipped away as he would want me to. I knew my husband well enough to know he despised appearing weak. To me he would always be Amenhotep, the Strong Bull Rising in Thebes; Amenhotep, Strong of Valor, and he yet lived. But for how long?

Sitting on the edge of the cushion, I listened intently to the girls' song.

> *Put one date in the basket*
> *Now put two*
> *Put one date in the basket*
> *None for you*
>
> *Put one date in the basket*
> *Eat it up*
> *Put one date in the basket*
> *Time is up*

At the end of their song they would laugh and start again. The sound reminded me of life long ago, living in the Algat tribe with my many sisters. How we had squabbled over the smallest thing, like ribbons and bits of rare glass. What fools we had been to mar our time together with such pettiness. I remembered their names and the sounds of their voices, but their faces were lost to me. I, Tiye, Queen of Upper and Lower Egypt, did not know if they lived or lay dead along with my son. I had been forbidden to communicate with my family, and wisely so. Huya alone could I speak to, but never of the Algat, or of home, or of our siblings. To do so was an offense against Amenhotep. What great favor and benevolence he had shown to me, reaching down from his throne and choosing me, a nobody, to be his Great Wife.

Walking to the balcony, I quietly listened to the girls' song as I daydreamed about the past. I had done this quite a bit recently, ever since the Desert Queen appeared in my court with her Red Lands clothing and her rough desert language. How I envied her the freedom she had enjoyed. I wondered how many sisters she had and if she would miss them as I missed mine. I smiled thinking of my sister Shaffar, the most beautiful and silliest girl ever born. I missed her most of all.

But I had been happy at times since those long-ago days. I had daughters of my own and even two sons, although it pleased Amun to steal one from me. My husband loved me above all women and had showered me with honors throughout our life together. Yet I did envy Nefret. I envied her freedom. The freedom to run with legs bare and arms wide. I envied her, and I would be the one to take that freedom from her as it had been taken from me.

I was the most powerful woman in Egypt, and I was a slave. A slave to a fate I had not sought or ever desired.

I thumbed away a rare tear as I listened to the girls sing a new song.

Fair of face,
Long of hair,
Isis beauty
Who can compare?

Spell her name…
Sacred bowl…clap, clap
Fan of pleasure… clap, clap
Fans of immortal winds… clap, clap
Hawk's fearless stand… clap, clap, clap

Angry bees rose up inside me. *How dare they sing praises to Kiya—spell her name, no less, and under my window! How dare they mock me so! Don't they know who I am?* In my rage, I grabbed a leather strap from a nearby table, walked out of my rooms and stormed down the marble staircase. Fearful servants and courtiers moved out of my way as I charged toward the group of girls who now stood in surprise. Without a word, I struck at them. They screamed in fear and pain, but I would not withhold their punishment. I swung the strap again, slapping bare legs and round bottoms. As young as they were, they had the good sense not to run but hunkered down obediently, covered their heads uselessly with their small hands and accepted my flurry of blows. They wailed in pain, and a crowd had gathered nearby, but not too near.

I continued to beat them until my wrist hurt and I could barely breathe. In my delivery, I had managed to strike myself a few times. One welt on my lower left arm looked particularly vicious. I was so surprised by the appearance of my own blood that I dropped the strap and glowered at the gaggle of wounded girls. Their skin was well striped with red marks now, but I saw no blood. Nobody raised their faces to me, but they cried all the same.

I turned my gaze to the people around me. They cast their eyes to the ground, except Huya, who stood as always nearly hidden against the wall. I summoned him with a wave and left the courtyard with Huya a few feet behind me. I would not retreat to my chambers or return to the harem; instead I made the long walk across the colonnade to my formal court to sit upon my blue throne. It amused me to do so and today, I needed some amusement. I almost smiled seeing the flurry of activity in the distance. I could hear the servants now: "The Great Queen is coming to her court! Make ready! Make ready!"

Yes, I needed to sit on my throne. It was my latest gift from Amenhotep and likely the last. The huge golden chair was covered with lapis lazuli, and my name was beautifully emblazoned across the back.

A shower of pink petals fell at my feet as I walked into the throne room. Two young slaves rushed before me with their baskets of flowers, careful to toss the flowers where I walked. As I approached the dais, they bowed low and disappeared from my presence, taking their baskets with them. Swinging my robes out of the way, I sat upon the throne and ignored my creaking knees. I held my back straight and kept my dark eyes fierce. The throne was so large and I so small, I had to retain this posture if I wanted to be taken seriously. Otherwise I would appear weak and ineffective, just a tiny woman wearing a crown that was never meant to rest upon her head. As was the tradition when the queen held court, my courtiers rushed into the chambers, still looking fearful and curious about what happened in the harem. Only the women had witnessed my outburst, but they would waste no time in recounting the event. Still, they would do so with respect. Of that I was sure. I smiled with pleasure knowing that I still struck fear into their hard, selfish hearts.

"My Queen, you are bleeding. Allow me to send for an attendant." My face a mask, I raised my right arm and watched the bright blood pour freely. I did not answer Huya, and I didn't need to. He always knew what I needed without my saying a word. Such a good servant was he that I sometimes forgot he was my brother. He shouted for a slave and whispered his request to her. I couldn't take my eyes off the glistening blood that now rolled down to my elbow. It had been so long since I had seen it. It had been many years since my lifeblood had flowed from between my legs. I watched in fascination as a drop of blood splashed onto my throne. I was not the only one to witness it. The gasp of the crowd broke the spell. I wondered at the sound when I heard a hoarse whisper from Heby, the ranking priest of Amun, at least for today. There was always a steady stream of new officials appearing in the courts of Amenhotep.

"Blood has been spilled on the throne. Royal blood! This is not a good omen. No, it is not." Heby's words traveled through the room quickly as my courtiers shared them with the onlookers. As quick as lightning, Huya sopped up the blood with a bit of linen. But before he could dispose of it, Heby stepped forward to collect it.

"The blood of the Great Wife is sacred, steward. You can trust me to dispose of it properly." Heby wisely kept his head down to prevent me from seeing the greed in his piggish eyes. No doubt he would use my own blood to work some obscene magic on me. Anything to raise the status of his pet cow, Kiya. He was the Mitanni woman's courtier, wasn't he? He raised his outstretched hands, expecting to receive the bloody cloth for whatever use he had in mind. How I would have loved to snatch Huya's blade and lop off Heby's grasping fingers! I was sorely offended by this exercise, but I could not refuse him. The priests of Amun held too much power over the people, and their confidence had been bolstered by the unredressed murder of my son not ten years ago. A day of vengeance would come for Heby and his brothers! But today was not that day. It was too soon, and my plans were not yet complete. I gazed at Huya, my eyes telling him what I wanted to say. Huya folded the cloth carefully and placed it in the fat priest's grimy hands.

I glared at Heby as he backed away with his unexpected treasure, his shiny head bobbing and glowing with excessive sweat and expensive oils. Quickly, before anyone else could claim my blood, Huya wrapped my arm himself, first rubbing stinging ointment on the skin. I didn't flinch but kept my eyes trained on the people, who watched curiously. As he tended to his ministrations, I studied the faces. Yes, I still had a few friends here, but only a few. I had been right to add to my retinue. The young, beautiful Nefret would certainly stir the pot. I noticed that Kiya had not bothered to appear before me, but I did spot her companion Inhapi.

"Inhapi, where is your mistress that she cannot attend me?"

"You are my mistress, Great Queen." She smiled pleasantly and nodded as she spoke, as if she were trying to convince herself of her own lies.

"I refer to Queen Tadukhipa." I didn't bother to return her empty smile. And then I added, "Some people call her the Monkey, but I prefer her proper name. Don't you, Inhapi?"

"Yes, Great Queen. I believe Queen Tadukhipa is tending to her daughter, Baketaten."

Beside me Huya whispered, "She is one of the children you punished."

I sneered down at Inhapi and said, "Well, go get her now. Her daughter can wait. Am I not the Queen of Egypt?"

"Yes, Great Queen." She backed away and left the courtyard to fetch the Hittite princess. How dare Kiya avoid waiting upon me?

"I see my daughter Sitamen, wife of Pharaoh, is here today. Tell me, Sitamen, what request have you for me? Have you brought me a present? I can see you have something in your hands."

"Greetings, Greatest of Pharaoh's Wives, Keeper of His Heart. I have indeed brought you a gift." I waved my daughter forward and waited to see what she would bring me. I studied her as she walked the processional to my throne. Taller than me by a head, Sitamen had the slim body of a maiden, a fair face and long, slender fingers. Draped across her arms was a wide silk ribbon in ivory and gold. Sitamen would have made a lovely queen, but alas for her, that would never be. She would never know the love of a kind spouse or feel the hard body of a man next to her, for she was of royal blood. She would die intact just as she had entered the world. My daughter bowed slightly and smiled up at me, offering her gift as she had when she was a child.

I examined it politely and touched the fabric, careful to keep my bloody finger from staining it. The gold stitching was clean and perfect, a simple motif of golden leaves wrapped around a resting snake. It was not a symbol that I recognized, and it likely had no significant meaning. Sitamen lacked the ability or desire to achieve any political goals. Of all the people in Upper and Lower Egypt, she was the least likely to rise up against me. I both loved her and loathed her at the same time. I sometimes wondered how I ever had given birth to such a passive child.

"Who sewed this ribbon, Sitamen? It is well done. It is good to have such a talented slave in your household."

"Oh no, Great Queen. No slave sewed this—this is my work. See the way the stitch is hidden along the seam? Memre says she has rarely seen any work so well made before. I made this for you. Perhaps you can wear it at the Sed festival. I would be honored to see you wear it...Mother," she added in her child's voice.

I withdrew my hand from the ribbon and sat up even stiffer. For the second time that morning anger burst from my belly. "What do you mean by sewing away like a slave? Do you think this is a proper activity for a royal daughter?" I heard snickering in the gallery but did not correct the guilty party. Sitamen needed to remember her place. She should feel ashamed for wasting her time on such menial projects. Sitamen's bright smile vanished, and she stood open-mouthed before me. That too made me angry. "No more of this. Next time bring me something of value, Sitamen." I dismissed her with a wave of my hand and looked for someone else to entertain me. How I longed to see an Amazon again or maybe one of the fair-skinned Pymere from the faraway northern lands.

"Great Queen, Aperel, the Master of Horse, has presented you with six new horses. They are in the courtyard now."

"Come forward, Aperel." I recognized the face. I had seen him many times in my husband's court, but this was the first time I'd had the chance to speak to him. He stood tall and straight and, despite his title, did not appear as if he had just stepped out of the stables. He wore a fine blue tunic with a collar of red stones. He was a handsome man with very few scars and a pleasing voice.

"Thank you for receiving my gifts, Great Queen."

"I thank you for the horses, Aperel. I cannot wait to see them."

"Whenever Your Majesty would like to see them, I will be happy to show them to you."

"Let us go now. I am anxious to see these fine gifts." I stood serenely, surveyed my court again and walked carefully down the dais. There was no one else with the potential to amuse me today. I extended my hand to Aperel, who bowed and blushed as I touched his hand. It was only a light touch, but I was sure that someone would mistake it for something more. Poor Aperel. Did he know what he was doing?

As we walked I encouraged him to tell me about the horses. How fast did they run? Who were their sires? Could they pull a chariot? I felt bored before he answered even the first few questions, but I enjoyed smelling his sandalwood skin and hearing his deep voice. He did nothing inappropriate, yet my mind wandered occasionally.

Oh, Amenhotep! My love! How long has it been since we have lain together as man and wife?

Aperel left me as I climbed the viewing gallery with my court. We watched the horses sprint, walk and parade for thirty minutes. It wasn't until the display was nearly over that Kiya appeared, looking very unhappy. With total disregard for protocol, she neither presented herself to me nor acknowledged me in word or deed. If my husband had witnessed such open abuse, he would have punished her severely. Her gaggle of ladies clustered around her, but they wisely bowed to me and repeated my name. Kiya waved her blue fan furiously as if she were in the midst of a heat stroke. Huya saw her too. I saw his jaw pop angrily at her affront. My brother was a proud man, prouder than even I was.

Poor unaware Aperel continued with his narrative until I finally stood and applauded. I had no idea how long this lecture would have continued without my interruption, but my stomach was rumbling and my mouth was dry.

"Thank you, Aperel. I shall tell Pharaoh of this generous gift. You have pleased me greatly." Aperel bowed low and whispered something to the horses, who also bowed the knee. I applauded again and laughed aloud at the trick. Looking again I could see one horse had failed to follow orders. Instead of bowing her knee she snatched her head away, proudly refusing to participate with the Master of Horse. He scolded and clucked at her, but I laughed again.

"What a wonderful trick, Aperel!" I called down from the galley. "I think you should name that one Tadukhipa—it does not have the intelligence it needs to know when to bow down."

The Master of Horse did not argue with me. He replied loudly, "Yes, my Queen. It shall be done."

I turned to leave the gallery but paused. My court paused with me. "On second thought, do not put such a burden on so beautiful a horse. We shall forgive her this time. I am not without mercy."

"You are ever merciful, Great Queen Tiye." Aperel smiled and bowed again.

With a snort, I fixed amused eyes on Tadukhipa, whose skin turned a deep shade of red—as red as the stones on Aperel's collar. Finally, I felt a small degree of satisfaction. As Huya filed in behind me, he winked but carefully kept the smile from his face. For as much as I hated her, Tadukhipa (or Kiya, the Monkey, as I liked to call her) was also the wife of Pharaoh Amenhotep. At any moment he could withdraw his great favor from me and make Kiya the Great Queen instead. And when my husband died and my son sat upon the throne of Egypt, how long would it be before she convinced him to do just that? He would inherit his father's harem, including the foreign queen who would waste no time in seducing him. Even now I saw her casting those longing looks in his direction.

This I would not allow. Whether she knew it or not, it was too late for Kiya. I had already chosen a wife for my son. A strong wife with the sand of the Red Lands in her veins.

All I had to do now was wait. I was good at that.

Chapter Two

The Stubborn Dead—Orba

Death had blazed through our camp with a mighty sword. A palpable spirit of grief loomed over us, and how cruel was the silence! The absence of the sounds of children playing heightened our sadness as we sheltered in the rocks of Saqqara waiting to hear if we would live or die. The Meshwesh spirit had been broken by the Kiffians, and now our fate hung in the balance. We were at the mercy of Egypt, and all our hopes were pinned on a girl who had never negotiated a trade much less pleaded a case in the courts of Egypt. Still, there was hope. As long as the breath of the divine rested in her, hope remained.

I felt a deep frustration that I could not see the future. I was not a fire-watcher as Farrah had been, although I knew her power had waxed and waned. Sometimes I could see glimpses in the water, like at the pool of Timia, but there was no water here in Saqqara. None that I had found yet, but I planned to continue searching for it, both for drinking and for seeing. Now that most of the Council had been murdered by the red-haired giants, there was only Samza and me left, and Samza had barely spoken a word since the destruction. The kings would ask my counsel, I assumed. And when they did, I would not let them down.

I stepped quietly into Semkah's small cave shelter. I was happy to see that despite his pain and fever, he was finally asleep. He had struggled to recover from his wound; the slice had been clean, but it had been difficult to protect the wound during our journey and now it festered. He had been a good king, much better by all accounts than his father had been. Leela smiled at me as she prepared a pot of food for the wounded king. I nodded and left her to her work. I had other matters to tend to.

I felt good about my decision to enlist the young woman's help. Leela had the potential to become a skilled practitioner in the healing arts but needed my tutelage. There were so few now who knew the Old Ways, I could hardly be choosy. Yet I recalled that Farrah had rejected the young woman for further training for one reason or another. And although we had once been lovers, Farrah did not seek my counsel in the matter or offer an explanation to me or anyone. Her solitary mind had been both her strength and her weakness.

I wrapped a black cloth around my head to protect it from the still blazing sun and walked through the camp. It was near dusk, and I welcomed the darkness and the relief from the heat.

All the tribes had come together. None had refused to rally with us, and that was a good sign, yet I felt unsteady. Whenever you had more than one king in a camp, tensions would rise. Especially now that our elected mekhma had been kidnapped and possibly murdered by the Kiffians and her rejected sister represented us. The camp was quiet; only a few women worked at cooking, and I began to notice that most of the men were nowhere to be found. Omel and his retinue were absent. This did not bode well. I squatted next to Ishna and asked her quietly, "Where are they? Where are the men?"

She tossed dried mushrooms into a brown liquid and pointed to the east without speaking. I reached in my pocket and removed a small pouch that contained a few pinches of herbs. "Here, Ishna. This is a good herb. It will give you strength." With a gap-toothed smile, the older woman accepted the pouch and looked around for something to give me. I dared not refuse her, for this was how we lived. We gave to one another, and there was as much joy in giving as there was in receiving. At least, that was the Old Way, the way both Ishna and I chose to live. She patted her neck and removed a leather necklace with an ivory pendant. She smiled again and handed it to me, and I examined the workmanship with an appreciative smile. "This is very nice. Thank you." Without a word but clearly happy, she stirred her food and sprinkled in some of the herbs.

Happy to have blessed the old woman, I left her to her food and walked purposefully in the direction she had indicated. I did not have far to walk and could hear Omel's booming voice before I saw him. He and the other kings were gathered in a rocky outcropping. Some were sitting and some were standing, but clearly it was Omel who led this meeting.

"Kings of the Meshwesh. From the beginning I have told you that Egypt was our true friend. And now you see that my words are true, although it pains me to say that my brother was wrong. I know our current situation worries many of you, but let me assure you that all will be well. As I have reported on many occasions, we have many friends in Thebes." Many of the men murmured, but nobody openly disagreed with him.

I paused behind the rock to listen to more of Omel's speech. I had always had my doubts about his loyalty to Semkah; now that the king was wounded and possibly dying, Omel no longer bothered to hide his true feelings.

"Even though generous offers were made to us in the past, you and I know that a king's heart, a Pharaoh's heart, can change."

"Get to your point, Omel." The voice belonged to Fraya, a southern king and distant cousin of Semkah and Omel.

"My point is this, brother. If you follow me as king, I will secure the deal we need. *I* can deliver Zerzura and Pharaoh's army. *I* have a powerful ally who will lend his help whenever I ask for it. If we leave this in the hands of the girl, we deserve to die here. Swear your allegiance to me, and I will ride out immediately. We have no time to waste."

"Make you king? We are all kings. Your brother sent the sigil—he summoned us here. We would hear from him on this matter," Fraya said, obviously unhappy with Omel's proposal.

"My brother is not well, King Fraya. In fact, he may not survive the loss of his arm. And even if he did, of what use is a one-armed king?"

"And what will this cost us, Omel? Are you thinking to give away our mines? That is all we have left."

Another man asked, "Will we have to give our daughters and wives to the Egyptians? I heard they prefer boys to girls. Will they demand our sons?"

Fraya calmed the crowd and asked Omel, "What promises will you make on our behalf?" It was clear that this man was not convinced.

"Deal-making is the art of kings, is it not? What makes you think my niece will secure us a better deal than I? She has not gone to Thebes to climb palm trees or shoot an arrow, yet you sent her to represent you. I counseled against this, but nobody listened to me. Now is the time to do something before we are undone!"

The kings sounded as if they were in agreement with Omel, and this was a dangerous thing. I chose that moment to reveal myself to the secret gathering.

"Hafa-nu, kings of the Meshwesh."

"Hafa-nu," they responded, surprised to see me.

"What are you doing here, Orba? I did not summon you."

With a scowl I answered, "You do not summon me, Omel. Nor do you dismiss me. I am a free man, as are all these men."

"Well then, little man, what do you have to say to us? Or have you come to tell us that my brother is dead?"

I was a small man, the smallest present, but I did not hunker down. Nor would I slink away merely because Omel pointed this out. I was no coward. I was no schemer like the man before me.

"Semkah is resting, and I expect him to make a full recovery. As I am sure you are happy to hear."

"My wife, who is a healer, says he will not survive. And even if he does, he will always have one arm. We have never had a one-armed king rule over us. My brother is a good man, but he cannot lead us like this."

"Indeed, we have never had a one-armed king. But then again, we still have a mekhma."

Omel snorted his disgust. "Nefret? She failed the trials, remember? Are you saying now that we should accept her when you yourself previously rejected her?"

"Ah, but she did not fail the last trial—she was unable to complete it. Or have you forgotten that our enemy murdered the tribe at Biyat?" To that he said nothing and only glared at me with his kohl-lined eyes. I continued, "However, I was not referring to Nefret. Pah is the mekhma. And until we know what has happened to her, she is mekhma still. It is acceptable to the Council if her sister held her place until we determine what has happened to her, but even then these things will not be decided like this!"

King Fraya rose to his feet and stood beside me. "I agree with Orba. If this is what the Council wants, then we will wait and see."

"The Council is only Orba and Samza. Are we to let these two men decide our fate?"

"Again you are correct, King Omel. Thanks to the Kiffians, only Samza and I are left, but I have taken steps to correct that. We are seeking new Council members from the Meshwesh, fresh blood to take the place of those we lost. I look forward to speaking with any whom you recommend, for I feel it is important that we keep the Old Ways. All tribes must be represented in our Council. This is what Farrah would want."

"And what does the Council say about Nefret? What is our future, Orba? What do our gods and ancestors say? What have you seen?" Fraya prodded.

The southern king eyed me hopefully. I felt the fate of our people resting on my skinny shoulders, as if Ma'at himself rode me, directing me. Here was a moment to instill hope—a rare moment given by the god. I could not miss this opportunity, yet I was not the kind of man who would lie to impress other men or to manipulate them to do my bidding. I had seen nothing yet, but a vision from many years ago sprang into my mind. As I recalled the details of the vision, I felt the warmth of the god's unction brewing in the pit of my stomach. The words came forth like water from a new spring, slowly at first and then more furiously the deeper I dug into it.

"A day of rejoicing approaches, brothers. A day like no other! We *will* walk the heights of Zerzura and see the sea again. The blue sea will lap our shores, and our children *will* rejoice that they live in a happy city. Oh yes, the sounds of children will echo in the streets! Our sons will grow strong and will wear our clothes, our colors. They will not wear the garments of Egypt, nor shall they be slaves to any man. Our daughters will marry our Meshwesh sons, and many nations will long to see their lovely faces. The bloodlines of our people will once again be sown with great seers and wise kings and leaders who will dispense justice and bring prosperity. In fact, the greatest king our people has ever known has yet to be born—but he will arrive and soon." I could see the face of the young man, a familiar face but one I had not yet seen. "Which of you shall father such a great son? This I do not know, but I do know there is one alive who will." Tears filled my eyes, and unexpected joy bubbled in my heart. I continued, "A mighty army approaches. But do not fear, Meshwesh, because your Deliverer has arrived. A girl with the power of Egypt in her hands! The falcon rises, and we ride upon its wings!"

The men listened wide-eyed at my prophecy, then cheered and hugged one another. All except Omel, whose angry countenance told me he neither believed me nor supported me. He was my enemy, and he would not soon forget that I had defied him. In fact, I had ruined his plan. I did not linger. I left the kings and walked down the trail to explore the caves. More than ever I wanted to find a clear pool of water so that I could seek the future. I knew every word of what I said was true, but now the hunger to see more drove me deep into the cliffs and caves. Like a thirsty wild hare, I scampered through one cave and then another seeking water. I imagined that I could smell it, which seemed improbable; I had seen no clue that there was any to find. It would be pitch black soon, and I didn't dare explore the caves in the darkness. These Egyptians liked their hiding places, even in death.

I looked back down the valley to the camp. I was very high into the cliffs now and could see the fires burning below. The smell of cooking meat made my stomach growl, and I was tempted to turn back when I heard a sound.

It was the sound of a woman singing. It was a pleasant and soothing sound. It came from above me, in a distant cave. I could see the faint light from a fire and was puzzled at the sight. As far as I knew no living person dwelt in Saqqara—this was the City of the

Dead, at least if you were an Egyptian prince. I was no such thing. Still, the sound of a woman's song intrigued me. Yes! I knew that verse!

Clumsily and without thought I climbed up the narrow path and then scaled the cliff, desperately hanging on with my cut hands and worn sandals. At last I lay panting on the cave floor. The singing ceased, but I could still see the light. I forced myself to stand. "Who is there?" No one answered, but I heard the sound of laughter. Yes, a woman's laugh. I nearly shouted when some small animal ran by my foot. Clutching my new necklace as if it were a talisman, I walked deeper into the cave until I saw her.

It was Farrah.

"My Orba. I was afraid you would not come."

"Farrah, what are you doing here? You are dead. I saw you with my own eyes. The Kiffians…" I fell to my knees and peered past the flames to see the woman I loved smiling back at me. Her hair was no longer white but brown again, just as it had been when we were young, when she let me touch it and kiss her. A desperate sob escaped my lips, and I said, "I am so happy to see you, even if you are only a dream."

"Tell me, Orba. Why have you come here to this lonely place? Ah…no need to explain. I see now. You want to see, don't you?"

"Yes. So much has happened, and I can't explain it all. I must know how to lead our people. Won't you help me, Farrah?"

With a slight movement of her hand she tossed something into the fire and the flames changed to purple. She invited me to look, but as always I could see nothing. "You know I cannot read the fire. What else can I do?"

"Go to the water then," she said impatiently. Even in dreams I disappointed her. Suddenly Farrah and her fire disappeared.

I gasped, nearly falling backward onto the stone floor. "Wait! Do not leave me, Farrah! I cannot do this by myself."

I sat in the silence of the dark cave, unsure what to do, when I heard a new sound: the sound of water. Using my hands to feel my way, I crawled deeper into the cave. My knee bounced on a sharp edge, and I winced in pain but kept crawling. A purplish light, like the one produced by Farrah's herb fire, appeared in front of me and shone down onto a small fountain that splashed at the back of the cave. So thirsty was I that I drank from the fountain without thinking. When I had drunk my fill, I splashed my face and sat patiently, staring at the water.

The water shone in the purple light, and in just a few seconds I could see images form before my eyes. As always seeing such things delighted and surprised me. I watched the face of Nefret appear; her red hair was gone, and in its place was a wig of dark braided hair. Upon her head was a crown—no, a double crown. Her lovely face vanished, and I saw another face: Omel's wife, Astora. She stood under the moonlight, her body nude and painted with magic symbols. She whispered spells, and as she spoke creatures poured forth from her mouth. Black, writhing creatures that crawled through our camp and wrapped themselves around many different leaders. "What can this mean?" I asked Farrah as if she would answer me. She did not.

Then I saw another scene. Farrah walked through our camp—this must have been around the day of the attack. She followed the child, the dead child, Nefret's treasure. The two walked into Pah's tent, but in my vision I was not permitted to enter. I saw Yuni storm out with an angry look on his ugly face, then Pah emerged, her robes covered in blood, a bloody dagger in her hand. I gasped at the sight. On a surge of foul wind I was carried inside the tent just in time to see Mina enter and issue a silent scream.

As Farrah took her last breaths I cried, "I am sorry, Farrah. We were wrong. It should have been Nefret. Now what do I do?"

Farrah appeared to me, wearing the same bloody robes, her hair white again and streaked with blood. She raised her hand toward me and pointed. "Now you see... You have seen the future, the present and the past. Now you see, Orba hap Senu. You will see in fire and water. Be mindful of your gift. Take no life, or you shall lose it."

In a soft flicker she disappeared, taking with her the purple light. With her she took all warmth from the cave. I had seen troubling visions. I crawled out of the cave as quickly as I could. I had to share all this with Samza.

We had a devious, evil enemy at work in our camp.

And soon we would be without a mekhma.

Chapter Three

The Song of Queens—Ayn

I knew what Omel was up to, and I stalked him nearly night and day. A man like him would never pass up the opportunity to sow discord. Until Nefret returned I would be her eyes and ears. I would not let her down in this. I watched covertly as Omel led his brother-kings out of our camp to the large rock circle to the north. So arrogant was he, so confident in his ability to coerce the other kings to partake in his rebellion, that he did not bother to hide his attempt at creating a coalition. I think he saw me once but paid me no mind. I had been labeled a liar. Who would listen to me now?

Still, I dogged his every step and did my best to avoid a direct confrontation. To her credit, Astora was ever observant and glared at me whenever we met. She knew I hated Omel, but she would probably never dream why.

Living in the Red Lands I had grown accustomed to hiding in plain sight, so even if Omel had bothered to occasionally glance over his shoulder he would have had a difficult time spotting me. My clothes were neither bright nor gay, and I wore no jewelry for I owned none. I could be as elusive as I liked. I frowned as he clapped his friends on the back and spoke in low, serious tones. If only I could hear the words! I heard the shuffling of pebbles behind me and flattened myself against a nearby rock. I slid my sword back into its sheath so the fading sunlight would not glint and reveal my hiding place. Slowly I turned my head to see who approached. I hoped it was Astora. I would love to confront the king's wife with the truth.

It was Orba! The little man was as loud as a blind goat. I considered getting his attention, but he did not look my way. Clumsily he paused as he sheltered behind one of the larger boulders in the Saqqara Valley. He was in the perfect position to overhear Omel's conversation. The rocky hollow in which they gathered created an amplifying effect. What fools men were! I removed my sword, my metal cuffs and anything that would clatter and laid them on the ground. I climbed the rock without detection and lay flat staring up at the sky as Omel began to make his case to the gathering.

He tried to be eloquent, but no words could hide the truth—at least not to me. Omel wanted to be king. It had been his lifelong ambition. I listened as he made insinuations about Nefret and felt hopeful when Fraya questioned him. Ha! This would not be an easy sell for the grasping Omel, Betrayer of Queens!

I warned Pah that her uncle could not be trusted long before she consummated her covenant with him. Even though the closeness of their association sickened me, I loved Pah even in her delusion. I had loved her deeply and even now scarcely let my mind wonder about where she was or what evils had befallen her. I loved her enough to hope she was dead and not suffering.

Pah and I had been childhood friends. I understood her and shared some of her feelings. As the only daughter of a mighty warrior with no sons, I felt the same rejection and witnessed my father's disappointment. Still I trained harder, fought longer and did everything I could to show my father that I had a warrior's heart. I don't think he ever saw it. Now he was dead, and I would never hear the words I so longed for. But Pah had seen it. She had commended me when I beat her at our daily races. She recognized my strength and insisted that I help her take her rightful place as mekhma. At the time, I had felt honored. Now I knew the truth. She had used me for her own ends and abandoned me when I needed her the most. It was the hard, bitter truth.

As I listened to Omel blather on, I thought about the daughters of Semkah. Until this past moon, I had not exchanged more than a few words with Nefret. I had believed Pah, who considered her sister weak and stupid. I related to Pah, who felt lost in the shadow of her radiant sister. The young women were very similar in appearance, but inside they were nothing alike. Pah had an endless need for affirmation—she had to be the best at everything. And when she wasn't, you saw the worst of her. She reminded me of one of the great cats, the black ones with huge marble eyes. Eyes that were wise and dangerous. Nefret was more like the falcon. She stayed aloof, above those around her. Not in an arrogant way, as I once supposed, but as one who must always look at the larger view. Pah was fierce and fast where Nefret was careful, even cautious. But Nefret had a wisdom about her that surprised everyone. What fools they had been—what a fool I had been—to lift up Pah as mekhma. The thought made me want to spit, but the heat of the rock dried my mouth and drained my strength.

When Orba made his appearance, I could hear the surprise in the council of kings. Ha! Such fools men were to let someone like Orba sneak into their midst unseen. And these were our leaders? Omel did not back down at first, but the power of Orba's prophecy disarmed him. I lay upon the rock and listened with tears streaming down my face. When had I last cried? I could not remember. I had not cried when Alexio whacked me with the flat of his sword. I had not cried when my father struck me in a drunken stupor, breaking my tooth and causing me to bleed for hours. I had not cried when I took the warrior's tattoos, although the pain had been almost more than I could bear. Now I heard the promise from the prophet's own mouth.

"A mighty army approaches. But do not fear, Meshwesh, because your Deliverer has arrived. A girl with the power of Egypt in her hands! The falcon rises, and we ride upon its wings!"

The hopelessness that I had carried with me to the top of that rock floated away. I believed Orba's words—I snatched them out of the air like they were living things and wrapped my faith around them. And I knew something else: I would serve Nefret for the rest of my days. That was all I ever wanted. To serve the mekhma, to offer my hands, heart and soul if required on behalf of my people. And even if she never recognized me or thanked me, these words would be enough. As Orba prophesied, Nefret would be our deliverer. She was the promised falcon. She would rise to the heights of power and would need someone she could trust. I had chosen poorly when I chose Pah, and I had failed Nefret once already by losing Paimu, but not again.

Wherever the mekhma went, I would go too—even if that meant traveling the far reaches of the Red Lands or traveling down into death. I would not allow Omel to abuse her as I'd seen him abuse Pah. When Nefret returned I would tell her everything! I heard the men below leaving their rocky fortress with encouragement on their lips. Whatever Omel's intention had been, this surely was not it. I stifled a laugh. I leaned up on my elbow slightly and watched them return to camp. The sun had gone down now, and the first, brightest stars appeared above me. The sky was the color of magic, somewhere between a deep purple and a blazing red. A streak of light slipped across the sky—a messenger of the gods, no doubt. It was an omen, but I did not ponder it. My heart was too full of hope to wonder at what tomorrow would bring. As I lay on the rock, my hands outstretched beside me, a song rose up from within me.

> *Hear now, Kings and Queens*
> *Warrior and Maid*
> *This is the tale of Nefret.*
>
> *She is the falcon that rises,*
> *Rises above the earth,*
> *She will lead us home,*
>
> *The City of White,*
> *The City of Little Birds.*

I did not wonder from whence the song came. My mother sang the songs of the gods, or at least she used to, and I heard them many a night when my father would go on long journeys along the trade route with his king. Songs such as these, spontaneous and magical, came unbidden from the gods, she told me. When I was a young girl, before I had breasts and before desire coursed through my veins, I sang too. But when it became clear that I would receive no love from my father Nari's hands, I abandoned the softness of music in favor of the unyielding, unloving metal of the sword.

I let the notes of my song fade on the breeze and then sang it over and over until I had memorized the tune and the words. This was not all...no, this was only the beginning of my gift to the mekhma, for queen she would remain.

As the air turned cool, I slid down from the rock and gathered my items, strapping on my sword and cuffs. I walked back to the camp, wondering who I would stay with tonight. There were only a few tents available; some families were hidden in the caves but even in the camp of the Meshwesh it was not wise for a woman to share a bed with a man. I had a few offers when we arrived but refused them all with a sneer. I needed no man's protection, for I had a sword and knew how to use it.

I decided to see if Semkah had food and wine, but to my surprise another tended to him. She was not from our tribe; perhaps she was from Omel's, but I couldn't be sure. She put her fingers to her lips when I entered, instructing me to be quiet. I stared at the king and watched him breathe for a few seconds before I left. I spotted a boy standing guard outside one tent. I had seen no one enter the shelter in the two days we had dwelt in Saqqara. I wondered to whom it belonged.

"You there. What is your name?" I stalked toward him authoritatively.

The young man, whom I did not recognize, could not have seen more than thirteen winters. He replied, "I am Amaktahef, but people call me Amak. How may I help you?" He was polite with bright eyes and dark brown skin, like the tribes from the west.

"Whose tribe do you belong to, Amak?"

"I am Siti's son. We are from Dahkia."

I saved him the trouble of asking me anything. "I am happy to see such brave young Meshwesh standing guard in our camp. Tell me, whose tent is this?"

He poked out his bony chest and raised his chin, somehow offended that I did not know. "This is the mekhma's tent. We keep it for her until she returns."

I smiled wryly. "And which mekhma are you waiting for, Amak?"

He thought about it for a moment and then answered confidently, "Whichever one comes back first."

I nodded but said nothing. There was no need to correct the boy. Pah was never coming back. She was dead or worse. But Nefret would return—he would see soon enough. "I am Ayn, the mekhma's guard. I will stay here until she returns."

He opened his mouth like a fish out of water. With a sigh I went into the tent and removed my sword, tossing it on the pallet. It was a small tent, but it would do. There were no fine trappings like cedar tables or hanging lanterns, not as when we stayed at Biyat or Timia, but it was better than climbing into bed with a grasping man. To my surprise, the boy followed me inside. I turned to face him and removed my cuffs. "Yes, what is it?"

"I just…are you sure? I don't want to get into trouble with my father. He said no one was to enter until the mekhma arrived."

"Did he now?" Curious and suspicious, I felt the hair creep up on the back of my neck. I picked up my sword and used the blade to shift the blankets around. No snakes slithered out, and no scorpions struck at the metal. After a few seconds, Amak's curiosity got the better of him.

"What are you looking for?"

"It is nothing. I thought I lost something. Tell me, Amak. Is your father a good man?"

"The very best man. He is good to all his children and his people." His grin told me that he believed what he said. This was not propaganda.

"Did he provide all this for the mekhma?"

"Yes, he did. He is a kind man, my father. He says she will return and lead us to Zerzura. It is a wonderful place. My father saw it when he was just a boy, and now he says I will see it. Have you seen it?"

"I have not, but we will. You tell your father that the mekhma's guard stands ready to serve him if he should need me." I put my hand on the boy's shoulder and looked down into his face. I was easily a foot and a half taller than he. "I am grateful for his thoughtfulness. It is good to know that she has friends."

A large smile spread across his wide face. "I will do so. Do you require anything? Perhaps I can serve you? I have been so bored standing here all day."

"Who bakes the best bread, Amak? A warrior needs food."

"Oh! My mother, the wife of Siti! I shall go now and fetch you bread and something to drink."

Amak didn't move but stood at attention.

"What is it?" I asked him, my stomach rumbling at the promise of food.

"Well, don't you have to dismiss me?"

Trying not to smile I said, "Very well, you are dismissed. Return quickly. No dawdling. And bring me an oil cloth for my sword when you return. And do not barge into the tent without announcing yourself first. I have a sword, Amak."

"Yes, Ayn." He scurried out of the tent, and I sat on the disturbed pallet, thankful for this happy turn of fortune. It was dark and getting darker. I opened a small box near the entrance of the tent and found a stub of a candle and a clay candle holder. I quickly stepped outside and lit the candle, returned and placed it in the candle holder. It wasn't much light, but it was more than many people had. By my estimation there were less than two thousand people in the Meshwesh camp; that was significantly less than the estimates had been before the destruction at Biyat. We lost many at Timia, but at least some of us had survived. Biyat's tribe would never walk the earth again. I opened the second box and found it full of Pah's things. I recognized her treasure box, and like a sneak I opened it. I picked up the small block of scented wood and sniffed it.

Oh, Pah. Why did it have to end like this? I pray you are happy in the life after. For some reason I felt compelled to place the items around the candle. I bent in front of them and prayed to my ancestors. I begged them to make Pah welcome, for she had once been mekhma. I prayed to the gods Ma'at and Hathor to forgive her for the evil deeds she had done. I pleaded with them to let her pass into the afterlife or send her back to complete her work. I ended my prayers and heard Amak outside the tent.

"Lady Ayn!" he called to me. "I am here with my father, Siti."

Rising to my feet, I eyed my sword but decided to leave it where it lay. There was a time for swords and there was a time for laying down swords. I could not kill a king, unless it was Omel. Him I could kill.

"Please come in."

Amak's arms were loaded with a basket. He began removing the contents hurriedly to the nearby crate, and I stood with a calm face watching Siti.

"Ayn, you are the daughter of Nari, aren't you?"

"Yes, my father was Nari. He is dead, killed at Timia."

"Sad day for us all." His brown eyes showed sadness as he continued, "The mekhma's guard is welcome to stay with us. We have an extra tent and are inclined to share our hospitality with you."

I couldn't hide my surprise. "I am honored, King Siti, that you would offer your hospitality to me. But my place is here. I will wait for Nefret to return."

"Please, it's just Siti. There are enough kings in this camp already. Speaking of kings, how is Semkah? No one will allow us to see him. As the mekhma's guard, surely you must know."

Ah, so there is a reason...

"I have just seen him. He is resting and has a devoted healer by his side. I am sure he will see you soon."

He breathed a noticeable sigh of relief. "For that I am grateful. Semkah is a good man, a true king. I would hate to discover that he had been mishandled." I could read between the lines: he did not trust Omel. I could not tell him that I felt the same way.

"I can assure you that if that were the case, I would not be standing here."

He had something else to say but before he could share whatever was on his heart, a noise rose in the camp. Shouts and sounds of battle. I reached for my sword and ran out of the tent toward the noise. *Oh, please, ancestors! Don't let it be the Kiffians! We are not ready!*

"Hold! Do not attack! Those are Egyptian flags! That is Nefret! The mekhma has returned!" Jubilation rose from the camp as Nefret galloped toward us, her red hair and green cloak trailing behind her. She rode the largest horse I had ever seen, black with a braided mane and muscled legs. Beside her rode a dark-haired man with a proud face, strong legs and broad shoulders. He was the handsomest and fiercest-looking man I had ever seen. He slid from his horse before it came to a good stop and ran to Nefret, helping her down as easily as if she were a feather. The cheers of happiness diminished as the sound of hundreds of horses' hooves pounded in behind them.

"Greetings, Meshwesh," Nefret called, settling down the retinue.

"Hafa-nu!" a woman called, and others echoed her devotion. "Hafa-nu, mekhma."

Nefret smiled and returned the greeting, "Hafa-nu, Ankanah. All will be well."

The people quieted after a few moments. They eyed the Egyptians suspiciously, but their souls leaped seeing that their brave queen had indeed returned. "This is Ramose, Pharaoh's general, and these men are Pharaoh's soldiers. They will do you no harm. They have brought us food—and weapons and all manner of things. Things we will need to make the journey home." As Nefret spoke I could not help but stare at the black-eyed man. Yes, his physique was stronger than any I had ever seen, but it was his sword that I could not tear my eyes from. It had a double edge and was made of a metal I had never seen before. The hilt shone in the firelight, and I could see a strange script on the glittering scabbard. He stared back, but only for the smallest of seconds.

"All will be well, Meshwesh. Do not be afraid."

"Hafa-nu, mekhma!"

She waved her hand as Farrah used to do. "Ayn!" She reached her hand toward me, and I hugged her as if she were my sister.

"Mekhma, I am glad you returned so soon. I was beginning to worry. Let me show you your tent. King Siti arranged a place for you."

We walked together and she whispered, "Siti? Tell me, what have I missed?"

"Quite a bit," I said sternly. "What did *I* miss? Are you a prisoner, then?"

"Hafa-nu, mekhma," the people greeted her as they passed. Some kissed her cheek, while others hugged her.

"Shh…we will talk more later. First, take me to my father, and then we will see what is what."

"Very well, mekhma."

"Please call me Nefret. I miss hearing my name."

Finally I had something to smile about. "Very well, Nefret. Come, he is just down here."

Chapter Four

The Snakes of Destiny—Nefret

Speaking to my father proved difficult, as many of my people wanted to touch me and speak to their mekhma. Thankfully, the hard-jawed Egyptian general did not follow me but set about his own tasks. I was happy about the absence of his company. During our frantic journey to Saqqara the tension between us did not lessen. Even though I was much younger than he, I could read him quite easily. He did not like me much and thought even less of his errand, but he would never speak against his queen. Still, if I had pulled back my covers at night and invited him in I knew he would have accepted my invitation—his eyes were ever upon my figure, especially my breasts. That was one invitation he would never receive.

Breathing a sigh of relief, I turned my attention to my treasures, my tribe. I didn't mind their reaching hands and greetings; providing them with some comfort and continuity of purpose was the least I could do. A young man with a ragged red wound across his face stepped into my path; his eyes were empty and feverish, and I suspected that his evil-looking cut needed attention. I recognized his face but did not recall speaking to him before this day. "Hafa-nu, mekhma. Are we going home now?" he asked in a weary voice.

"What is your name? I know you."

"Biel, the son of Jeru."

"Yes, Biel. We are going home to Zerzura." I clasped his hands in mine and looked directly into his eyes. "Very soon. You rest now, Biel, and get your strength back. Find a healer to tend to that wound. We will need your help, and you must be whole and well."

He didn't argue but asked, "What of Alexio? Will he not return with us? I could track him, mekhma. He taught me how. I am sure I could find him."

I gulped at hearing my husband's name, for in my heart he was that still. In an angry moment I had cast him out, sending him on a fool's errand. How would Alexio retrieve my sister from the Kiffians by himself? I had behaved like a jealous shrew and had likely sent him to his death. I wished that I myself could climb upon a horse and pound the hooves to seek him out, but my place was here. My desire for him was strong, and my heart was breaking, but there was nothing I could do. Sending this boy into the desert would achieve little except kill another innocent. Despite his lion's heart, Biel hap Jeru was in no shape to travel the four corners of the desert. I could not have his death on my conscience. However, perhaps I could ask Ramose to send a squadron of men to find him. That would certainly not be inappropriate, as he was sent to serve me. I did not look forward to asking Ramose for anything beyond his required duties, but for Alexio I would face the giants myself.

"Alexio has gone to find my sister. He will return to us soon, I am sure of it. Rest, Biel, and regain your strength." He did not look happy with my answer. "I have not forgotten Alexio. We will bring him back."

His empty eyes brightened for a moment, and he squeezed my hands and stepped out of my way. Others flooded in, needing my assurances, handshakes and hugs. Ayn remained by my side but did not dissuade them. Finally, I gave her a look that said, "Help me." Without a word, she stepped between my people and me and grasped me by my elbow.

"Come now, mekhma. Semkah awaits." With each touch of their hands, I felt a weightiness and solemnity that I had never experienced before. By the time I had pushed my way into my father's abode, I was emotionally drained and desperate to see his face.

"Greetings, mekhma. Your father is resting now," a tiny young woman said as she stirred a mixture in a bowl.

"Who are you?"

"Leela. Orba asked me to look after the king. As I said, he is resting now. Although I don't see how with all this noise. I have given him a sleeping potion and must apply this poultice to his stump."

I didn't know what to think of Leela, but before I could argue with my father's caregiver, I heard the voice I had so longed for.

"Nefret. Thank the gods. Come. Please, Leela, step out of the way." He was trying to sit up without the use of his right arm. It was a disheartening sight, but I did not try to help him. He would not welcome my assistance or sympathy. When he pulled himself up, his appearance shocked me. He had looked weak and near death's door before I left, but now his skin had taken on an ugly yellow tone, his eyes were red and his frame was gaunt. I masked my surprise and answered him with as much confidence as I could muster.

"Yes, Father. I am back, and Egypt is with us."

"Leave us," he said to the other women.

Without argument they left, although Leela did not hide her disapproval. "I need to apply this poultice while the medicine still has its effectiveness."

"Out," he growled. Once we were alone he reached his hand out to me, and I squeezed it. "I think she is going to poison me with her concoctions," he said sourly.

"I think she is trying to *help* you, and for that I am thankful. Are you feeling well?" I didn't know how to ask what I wanted to know. *Are you going to leave me too?* I could not bear it if after all this I lost him too. Without him, I would have no family left. My treasure, Paimu, was dead. Pah had been stolen from us, and now…

"No tears for me, Nefret. We have no time for that. Tell me everything that has happened. Do not leave anything out. Not even the smallest details."

"I hardly know where to begin. Queen Tiye rules in Egypt. I never laid eyes on Pharaoh or entered the main palace. There is nothing done that she does not know about."

"There have been rumors of this for a long time." With a worried look he added, "Were you presented to any other members of the court? What about the son—the heir?"

"No, Father. I met no one else. Only the queen's steward, Huya. I attended no formal affairs and did not leave the queen's chamber except for bathing and dining. They do much of both, but I was kept mostly to myself unless the queen chose to visit me."

"Tell me about her, daughter."

"I really know nothing at all. She is a small woman but has a great presence. She reminds me of Farrah in that regard. She trusts no one and does not much talk to others except for her steward."

"What did she ask you about? Did she ask about your sister?"

"No, Father. She asked about our people, our festivals, our trade. She was curious to know our stories and songs. I told her many during my stay."

"Curious. Whatever her reasons, it seems you are now the queen's new favorite. You tell your stories too well, Nefret." I didn't know what to say to that, so I said nothing. All I had wanted to do was survive and receive the help we needed. He squeezed my hand and said kindly, "I do not blame you. I will miss you when you leave me, Nefret."

I breathed a sigh of relief. He knew. He must have known all along that I would have to leave him. I would never have imagined that my journey to Egypt would end in such a way. I bent down, kissed his forehead and wiped the tears from his eyes. "Who knows, Father? Perhaps the queen will allow you to come visit me. Maybe she will change her mind. Who knows what the future holds?"

He reached up with his good arm and pulled me close to him. My hair fell around us like a curtain, and we shed tears together. Finally he pulled my forehead to his and whispered, "You will always be mekhma, and you will always be my daughter."

"Semkah!" my uncle called from outside the tent.

"Help me up."

I did as he asked and pulled him to his feet. He wobbled, probably from the effects of the potion Leela had administered. "You must sit, or you will fall down," I said. "Here, sit on the edge of the table."

Father eased himself down on the table, and I quickly threw a cloak over his right shoulder to conceal his wounded arm. He pulled it around him and said, "Come."

"Greetings, brother. It is good to see you well." Dressed in his battle gear, Omel looked quite the king. He wore a leather breastplate with the tribe's sigil carved into the chest. At his arms were Corinthian leather greaves, but the rest of his garments were in the Egyptian style.

"I am hardly well. Nefret was just sharing her report with me. Please continue. You were telling me their terms."

"Yes, I am curious to know that as well. What did we exchange for their help? The gold mines of Abu Simbel? Queen Tiye would be a fool to take less."

Hesitantly, I shook my head.

"The turquoise mines, then? What is it? As you've said many times, brother, Egyptians do not offer their help for nothing."

"The Great Wife, for that is what she is called in Thebes, graciously sent a legion of soldiers, food for our journey and supplies in exchange for my promise."

My father and uncle waited to hear the words. "Promise of what?" Omel asked warily.

"After the conquest of Zerzura, I am to return to Thebes."

"What made you agree to this? Do you know what this means, Nefret? For what purpose? Are you a prisoner? This is an outrage! Call the kings together now, Semkah."

"The deal is done, Uncle. It cannot be undone. General Ramose is here now with orders directly from the queen's own steward. Do you think this is what I want? No, of course not, but as the Egyptians say, it is now written in stone."

"What is Queen Tiye thinking?"

"I do not know the queen's mind, for she keeps her own counsel, but this was the only deal she would make. She would take nothing else. I am to return to Thebes after the conquest, and she says that I can never return home again."

"This can only mean one thing. She intends to give you to her son," Omel said with a sardonic grin.

"What?" I couldn't help but blurt out. "Give like a concubine?"

"Maybe. If you please him, perhaps as a wife. But those kinds of arrangements are usually made more diplomatically with royal daughters who have large dowries. I see no advantage to her in raising you to that exalted position. However, it is possible, for it is Pharaoh who has the last word in those things."

"Uncle? Did you know about this?"

"How could I? This was your idea, mekhma."

Memories of consummating my union with Alexio under the full moon filled my mind. How could I be given to another when I belonged to him? And I had sent him away! What would I do?

My uncle continued, "I would say the Snakes of Destiny have been at work here. I had no hand in this. Would you be surprised to know that Queen Tiye herself was a commoner and had no royal lineage when she came to the throne? Amenhotep did not listen to the priests who had another in mind. He would have no one but the dark queen. They sometimes call her that because of her skin and maybe because of her dark moods. She is a dangerous woman if you cross her. I know for a certainty that Queen Tiye has put whole families to the sword, all in the interest of protecting her lineage. Perhaps she has a softness for desert folk. I would never speak this to another soul, but the Great Wife is rumored to be from the Algat tribe."

"Is this true?" My father sounded amazed by this revelation.

"Yes, but do not repeat that to a living soul—especially an Egyptian, and especially her general. By the way, Ramose has requested to be presented to you, Semkah. Shall I send for him?"

Ignoring his question for the time being, Semkah looked at me and asked, "What of this man? You have spent time in his presence. Is he trustworthy? Has he revealed the route to Zerzura to you?"

"I never learned to read maps, Father, nor was I shown one. But from what I understand, the city lies to the north, very near the sea. It is between Barrani and Matru."

"Do you trust him?"

"He is loyal to the queen. He will do as she has ordered him."

"Very well. It is late, and I am sure the general is tired from his journey. Brother, please send my thanks to the general and tell him the mekhma and the kings of the Meshwesh will meet with him in the morning. We have much to talk about."

Omel made the sign of respect and walked out of the tent. I could not help but notice the smirk on his face.

What will happen to the Meshwesh when I am gone?

Almost as if he could hear my thoughts, Father said, "That is enough worry for one day. Go rest, but come early in the morning. We will break our fast together, and I will summon Orba as well to see what can be done about all this." With a wince he said, "Tell Leela to return to me."

"You don't want me to stay? I can take care of you, Father."

He frowned disapprovingly. "You are the mekhma. I have everything I need."

I didn't argue and remind him that I was also his daughter. This was a matter of pride. I made the sign of respect before leaving.

"When you return in the morning, bring Ayn. Keep her close. She will protect you."

"I will, Father. Good rest." I slipped out into the darkness. Ayn sprang to her feet and walked beside me. I suddenly felt tired, more tired than I had felt in a long time. Even though the tent would not have all the comforts I had grown accustomed to, I would at least be among my people.

"Just this way."

Most of the excited welcomers had gone to their own tents and caves to prepare for rest, but many would sleep with one eye open. They would probably not see the Egyptians as allies, so I would have to be the example to keep the peace. I had no doubt that even now my uncle was thinking about how to use this situation to his advantage.

"Are you hungry, mekhma?"

"Not really, but I am thirsty."

"You rest now. I'll go find something for you to drink."

"Please, no wine. I had enough in Thebes. Water will do nicely." Ayn left me to take care of her task while I undressed. Someone had been kind enough to unpack my bag, and I found my robe and the few other items I managed to salvage from Timia stashed in the tent. I had little else in the way of clothing, but thankfully some thoughtful person had left me a nice soft tunic for sleeping. I tossed off my cloak and slipped out of my sandals and tunic. I noticed the small shrine that had been erected to my sister. Pah's cedar box had been emptied and each item placed around the stub of a yellow candle. I felt a lump rise in my throat. *Sister!* My mouth felt dry, and my feet and hands felt dirty, but I was so tired that I lay down and fell fast asleep.

The next thing I remembered was seeing a spiral appear before me. It reminded me of the whirlpool at Biyat, the one that Pah and I used to toss dried leaves into and then watch them sink away from sight. I watched the spiral with fascination as a bright blue light began to emanate from the center. Although the color resembled hot flame, I felt neither heat nor any other sensation from the spiral. I reached toward it, tempted to poke my finger at the very edge just to see for myself what this thing was before me. I became aware of whispers in the air around me. The closer my hand came to the spiral, the louder the whispering became. It was as if there were a crowd of people excitedly watching my every move. Without moving my head, I glanced to the left and to the right, but I saw no one and nothing.

I surveyed my surroundings. I was in a room—a spacious room with no walls, no doors and no floor or ceiling. It was very dark except for the spiral that spun in front of me. The air crackled, and I felt the hair on my arms rise just as if a thundering storm approached on the horizon. I put my hand toward the moving circle again, and this time I touched it. Nothing happened. I pulled back my hand and examined my finger. I had not been burned or scarred at all. I touched it again, tracing the edge of the spiral, and with some delight watched the light bend underneath it. The more I touched the spiral, the faster it spun. Soon I used my palm to spin the spiral until it was moving so fast that it was only a bright blue blur.

I became aware that someone was standing beside me. I did not feel threatened or afraid, so I spoke to the man. "What is this?"

"Look closer."

I did as the man instructed me. Leaning my head forward a little, I peered hard at the spiral, but the speed at which it turned made it difficult to see anything. As if he heard my thoughts, the man reached out and slowed the spiral to its original speed. In the center I could see figures—people I knew! There was Farrah and Paimu. Then I could see many of the Meshwesh who died in the Kiffian raid on our camp. I gasped at the sight. It was as if I were watching the memories of my past in very great detail, not at all like a dream. The man touched the spiral again, and the picture changed. I no longer saw people I knew but people I would know. I saw children, children with my eyes and dark hair. I saw a man's hands. He placed them on the heads of my children and spoke a blessing over them. I could see a boy's face. He had the look of my father but with eyes like mine.

Smenkhkare! I whispered. How I knew his name I did not know, but my heart reached for him. It claimed him as my own.

The man touched the spiral again, and the movement turned the spiral in the other direction. I saw my face now. I was standing at the top of a stony mountain. I appeared as an old woman with deep lines on my face and white hair. Below me in a valley I could see and hear sheep, many, many sheep. I saw my people, but they weren't my people. In some ways they appeared as Meshwesh, but they were taller and stronger looking. I heard someone shout my name, but it wasn't my name.

I turned to ask the man what this all meant, and for the first time I could clearly see—this was the Shining Man! His face was shrouded in light, but I felt that he was smiling at me.

"What does it mean? Who were those people?" I felt a wave of love, but he did not answer me right away. "Who was the boy?" *Smenkhkare!*

"You will meet him one day, if you choose to follow that path."

My heart pulled toward the boy in a way that I had never experienced before except with my treasure, my Paimu. I loved him purely and completely, yet I did not know him. But I did know I was willing to die for him.

"I must see him. This I know."

He smiled again, and this time the light moved so I could see his features. He had a long, straight nose and dazzling eyes made of every color imaginable. A light shone from his skin, yet he was not frightening.

"Then the path is chosen. Walk in it." He placed his hand on my head just as I had seen the man bless his children in the spiral, and I was filled with warmth.

I fell into a deep, restful sleep.

Chapter Five

An Immortal Name—Ramose

Another day in this stinking camp and I would go mad. These tribe-folk and their incessant drum-banging and off-key singing gave me daily headaches, and my impatience with my current situation was growing. The preparations took days longer than I had originally expected. The Desert Queen insisted that the entire clan make the journey with us as we progressed to the north. Obviously the girl had no idea how to lead an army or a campaign. But contrary to what she might think, her opinion had been of little importance to me. I had my orders.

In the end, I ignored her command and messaged Nebamun of the Third Legion. He would advance on Zerzura, remove the inhabitants and send an immediate report on his progress. Much of the battle would be over by the time we arrived at Zerzura, but I gave him explicit instructions to leave some of the Kiffians alive for appearances' sake. These Meshwesh "kings," as they fancied themselves, would not be denied their glory no matter how false that victory was. And who was I to say otherwise? Only the general of the Egyptian army. I snorted as I rubbed the leather of my greaves with cedar oil.

The Desert Queen would not be pleased, but I did not serve her. Besides, I was anxious to return to Egypt. What was once court gossip had proven to be true, according to my wife, Inhapi, who was Queen Tadukhipa's closest confidante. Amenhotep, Father of Egypt, lay dying. As his general I needed to be by his side, not babysitting a minor queen who struck the fancy of old Queen Tiye. I wondered what the Great Wife had in mind for the girl, but I was not one to worry much about such things. Inhapi did that for me. Once I finished oiling my leather, I polished my blade until it gleamed in the firelight. When I left this stinky hole, I would leave as a son of Egypt, not covered in sand and goat dung. I would make my Pharaoh proud. Like all intelligent men, I feared him, but I loved him too. He had been good to me over the years, granting me whatever I wanted. He had proved a crafty and intuitive leader, but battles had been few during his peaceful reign, and I longed for a decent battle. Perhaps that was why this delay seemed so unfair. I hadn't wet the edge of my blade with the blood of my enemies in some time, except for the necessary executions specifically assigned to me. But what sport was there in lopping off the heads of whining courtiers?

I tried to share these thoughts with Inhapi, but she did not care to hear them. "Why must you question everything? Amenhotep does you great honor by asking you to do these things."

"Yes but I am the general of the Egyptian army—not the chief executioner."

Inhapi's dark eyes flashed at me, and the beads of her expensive wig clicked as she snapped her head around to glare at me. "Then what do you want, Ramose?"

"An immortal name—as any man does," I had answered her, but she waved her hand at me as if I were the stupid slave who had arranged her many silk gowns in the wrong order. My wife would never understand my mind, but I did know hers. She had a lovely face, came to the marriage bed with great wealth and was more ambitious than anyone other than Queen Tadukhipa. I agreed with Nebamun. Men were stronger and more intelligent than women, but in matters of wisdom and ambition, the fairer sex far exceeded their male partners. I was often amused and equally annoyed by the conversations Inhapi had with Tadukhipa. I warned them to keep their schemes to themselves, but they merely laughed.

An intense argument nearby pulled me from my daydreams. I smiled at the sound of the Meshwesh father confronting our soldiers for some conceived wrong. If this continued, I would have to make my suggestion concerning the tribal women an official order. The truth was my men were bored. And when soldiers are bored, they tend to get into mischief. That mischief usually involves drinking excessively or indulging in another sport, women. Because there was not much beer or wine available, the Seventh Legion concentrated on the latter. I warned them to keep their hands to themselves—these desert mongrels would hate to have Egyptian sons-in-law—but these were not boys, and I was not their father. These men had been promised a battle with the Kiffians, a long-hated enemy of the two kingdoms.

"Greetings, General Ramose."

"Horemheb." I eyed the Meshwesh king suspiciously. Here was another one I could do without. "Do you bring an order from your Desert Queen?"

I pretended not to notice his grimace. I could read him well enough to know what he thought about the girl who ruled over him. He was a proud man and had schemed greatly to get the advantage over his brother—

all to have the kingdom stolen from him by his own niece. And not the niece he intended either. I found great humor in that and did not bother to hide my amusement.

"I am not a messenger, Ramose. I do not deliver orders."

I grinned and slid my sword into its sheath and set it beside me. "My apologies, then. Why have you come, Horemheb?" The tall man dawdled about as if I could discern his thoughts by merely watching him shift his feet. "Out with it."

Without being invited, the tribal king sat near me close to the fire. I did not care for his proximity but made no mention of it yet. I've always found that you should never refuse information when it is presented to you, and Horemheb looked like someone who might be willing to part with some.

"The kings will meet with you in the morning, in my brother's cave."

"You could have sent a servant to tell me that. Yet you come. What else have you to say?"

I have always dealt fairly with Egypt. You know I have come many times to Pharaoh's court on behalf of my people; I have long desired stronger ties with the Black Lands."

"Yes, you have frequented Pharaoh's court." He appeared to need encouragement to continue, and I hoped my agreeing with him would serve that purpose.

"You know I am a wealthy man, General. The gold mines of Abu Simbel belong to me only. My brother has no claim to them. Of all the men here, I am the wealthiest."

I tossed my last piece of firewood on the waning flames and waited. I could have corrected him by sharing stories of the wealth I had acquired during my service to my Pharaoh, but why bother? His self-importance amused me.

He licked his thin lips and prattled on. "I am not a greedy man. I reward my friends. Help me claim my right, and I will gladly reward you, Ramose. For a man of your skills, what I am asking is a small thing. My people need a strong leader—someone who values Egypt. Not an impetuous young woman who will doubtless embarrass them and worse, lead them into danger. She is too inexperienced, a spoiled princess with a weak father who does not respect Egypt. As king, I would always put Egypt first."

Was he asking me to kill the girl? A smirk spread across my face. "You have asked me nothing as yet, Horemheb, but let me remind you that I am here at the Great Wife's command. I obey her above all others, except for Amenhotep. So unless you have a request from him regarding your 'small thing,' then perhaps you should stop speaking. And if I may be so bold..."

He drew his wiry frame up and glared at me but wisely kept his mouth shut.

"You do not know me so well that you could ask me to do murder for you, if that indeed is what you ask of me. If I were not man enough to kill when I needed to, I would not lower myself to ask another to do the work for me. For that would make me less than a man."

He rose to his feet like a viper had struck his calf. My hand flew to my sword, and a nearby lieutenant set his hand on his khopesh and waited for the man to make the wrong move.

Horemheb stalked off through the sand, and I breathed a sigh of relief. It would do no good to kill one of the tribal kings before I took their mekhma away. The lieutenant laughed mockingly in Horemheb's direction and went about his business. I picked up my sword and strode to my tent. I had had enough of these people for one night. I thought about calling the captains to my tent to review our plan of approach, but we had been over it three nights in a row. It was time to move this bleating, banging tribe to their permanent encampment in Zerzura. And good riddance! From what I heard, it was not the holy land they expected it to be. Then again, what city could compare to Thebes? I had expected to hear something from Nebamun today, but as of yet no messenger had arrived. Perhaps the best thing would be to rest and steer clear of any of these Red Lands dignitaries.

"General," a female voice called from outside the tent. Who could that be? There were no camp women here. Perhaps the Desert Queen had come to her senses after all. I slid back the flap and found myself face to face with the Desert Queen's guard, Ayn. She was as tall as me, but I noticed she had not come dressed in her warrior garb tonight. Rather, she wore a long, soft-looking tunic, and her wavy hair was brushed to a shine. I caught a whiff of her scented skin as I held the flap back to invite her in. I looked about as she ducked inside to make sure none of my men saw my visitor.

"Ayn, isn't it? What can I do for you?"

She didn't answer me right away but instead strolled to my table of weapons. I added the sword I carried to the collection and watched her survey my inventory. "Do you need a lesson in weaponry?"

"Do you think I need a lesson in weaponry?"

I stared at her. I was too tired to play games. "Speak plainly, then. What can I do for you? Are you here in service to your mekhma?"

"No." Her voice sounded rough and serious. "I am here for myself." She stepped toward me, and I studied her. She was not a beautiful woman, but she was attractive. I was a man who admired strength in others, and it was rare to find it in women. Her arms were well made, the muscles sculpted from her warrior's work. Her breasts were small, and she had a slim figure without any woman's curves. I could tell she had never borne children, for her hips were straight and slim. Even in her soft brown tunic I could see that her skin was clear and perfect. She stood quietly and let me appraise her. I noticed with some amusement that she was studying me too. That thrilled me, and I felt my manhood rise.

I stepped closer to her, putting my finger under her chin to stare into her eyes. They were brown and warm like the eyes of a doe. Yet there was no fear in them. Her most attractive feature was her lips, bare, pink and full. I imagined them suckling on various parts of my body but doubted that she had the skill or knowledge to please me in such a way. Perhaps she would allow me to teach her.

"Are you a gift from your queen?"

"I am no man's property. What about you, General? Are you someone's property?"

I gripped her forearms and pulled her close. I saw no fear, only curiosity and desire. My answer was a rough kiss. If she fled from me, I would know she was not worthy of me. But she did not.

Ayn kissed me back, and her frenzied hands ran over my chest. I stripped off my garments and stood before her in my naked glory. With a serious face, she unbound her hair and untied her tunic, letting it hit the floor. Looking at her pleased me, and as we came together I cupped her breasts in my hands. We feverishly kissed again and to my surprise she pushed me down onto my bed. Her dark brown hair fell across my face as she scooted onto my lap. She said nothing, and neither did I. No promises were made, no lies were told. Ayn had come for one reason, and I was obliged to give her what she wanted. I massaged her breasts as she moved in perfect rhythm until I could take no more. I arched up and flipped us, and she struggled with me, perhaps disappointed that she was no longer in control. But after a few minutes she began to shudder beneath me. I rode the crest of the euphoric wave and plunged into her one last time, then fell on her hair and breathed in her scent. She smelled of cedar, some unknown flower and sweat. It was a pleasant combination and a far different one than that of the women of the Egyptian court.

I collapsed beside her. She did not linger long. The dusky-skinned girl collected her tunic and tied her hair. The oil lamp sputtered, and the light flickered.

"Did you get what you came for?" I asked her playfully.

I could feel her observing me in the darkness, but she did not answer me. Ayn ducked out of the tent and left me with my thoughts. So sleepy was I that I did not think of anything much. I drifted off and slept through the night.

Chapter Six

The Gift—Nefret

We rode hard for the walls of Zerzura. After seeing the palatial estates in Thebes and the brightly colored walls of the Egyptian temples that lined the city's roads, Zerzura appeared diminutive in comparison. But to most of my people, it was the reward of a generation of prophecies, and they would not be denied. Smoke billowed from behind the stone walls, and the grand wooden doors were firmly closed against us. Behind Zerzura was a steep line of hills and beyond that the blue waters of Mare Nostrum.

Ramose ignored my request to wait for the Shasu, the most elite warriors of the Meshwesh, and sent another legion of his soldiers to Zerzura to take the city by themselves. In no way did I want Egypt to claim the victory. Everyone knew that what Egypt took, it would not give back. We had not come all this way to be living out of Egypt's hands.

The only reason I did not send Ramose back to Egypt was that he agreed to send scouts to find Alexio. I had told him, "I sent one of my most trusted advisers to track my sister, but that was some time ago. I need someone who knows these lands to bring him back, with or without her."

"Who is this man to you?" he had asked me suspiciously, looking from my face to Ayn's as he munched on one of the last remaining apples.

"Is that important?"

"I think it is, mekhma. My mission, and that of my men, is to provide you with assistance. To take your people back to your homeland. And of course, to keep you protected until we return you to Queen Tiye's protection. I heard nothing about traveling the desert searching for anyone—even a trusted adviser. How is that pertinent to my orders?"

Ramose had peered at me as he squinted into the sun that morning. It rose behind me, and I felt its warmth upon my bare neck. He was wasting my time—I knew he did not want to help me, although Ayn seemed to think differently. I suspected that my guard was smitten with the arrogant general. Regardless of this potential conflict of interest, I knew I could trust her. But I would never trust him.

"It will be difficult to leave my people without Alexio here. He is a voice of reason and knows his father better than anyone. The people need him!"

Ramose had handed the apple core to his white horse and scoffed, "The people need him? I am not so certain. There seem to be a great many kings around this place. Surely the Meshwesh can live without one more leader." He closed the distance between us, but I did not flinch. "Be warned, Desert Queen, I will not allow you to break your promise to the Queen."

My brows knit together, and I dropped my voice menacingly. Ramose wasn't the only one committed to this mission, as he called it. "I have no intention of breaking my promise. Despite what you think, I am a woman of my word."

With a disrespectful glance he murmured, "Hardly a woman at all," as he turned to walk away. I wished I had a knife in my hand.

Ayn shouted, "Do not turn your back on the mekhma! Her request is not unreasonable, General! Unless it was your intention all along to leave the Meshwesh at the mercy of Omel." She leaned on her spear, and her voice was stern—even angry at Ramose's disrespect.

"Omel?" He spun on one foot. "You mean Horemheb?" We had his interest now. "What does he have to do with this?"

I replied, "Alexio is his son and my closest ally, except for Ayn and perhaps one other. His presence here is crucial if we want to keep the people safe."

"Safe from what? Egypt? You will owe her your life before this is over."

I didn't back down. I needed his help, and I felt his resolve weakening. "And how will the Queen view this decision, General? After all the expense? All the time invested? I do not know her well, but I believe the Queen to be a shrewd woman who is accustomed to getting a return on her investment. What will she think when you have to return to this region—to Zerzura—because Omel, or Horemheb, as you call him, has sold the gold mines to the Greeks? Or better still, the Mycenaeans, who are always hungry for the metal?"

With an angry shout of frustration, Ramose had walked away, but Ayn reported to me that evening that he had indeed sent out a small scouting party to bring Alexio back.

On top of my request, Ramose had not taken kindly to the idea of waiting for the caravan to snake its way through Saqqara and the Red Lands—he had made that plain enough. In the end, the Shasu and the Egyptians led the second attack but did not get very far. The initial attack had done little except alert the Kiffians that we intended to retake the city. The Third Legion had arranged themselves in front of the four towers of the White City, but there was nothing we could do except wait on a better plan.

"This was a mistake!" Amir, the leader of the Shasu, complained to Omel, who stood beside me. "What now?" The canopy was full of tribal kings, including my father, my new ally Siti, Orba, Ramose and two of his men whose Egyptian names escaped me. Ayn and I were the only women present. All eyes were on me.

"Amir, I know you are anxious to avenge our fallen brothers and sisters, and for that I thank you. But now we must work together. We are too close to victory."

General Ramose said, "The fastest way to deal with these savages is to burn them out. A few well-placed fires and they will scream for mercy."

"And destroy our city?" Orba asked him as if Ramose were a child asking to play with a basket of asps. "What happens when you leave and our defenses are down? We will be at the mercy of any who decide to come against us."

"We have used this method before, at the Wall of the Crows and at Kadesh, and those walls were much taller than these. My men can position the flames in a manner that will minimize the damage. Once the city is yours, you will have all the time you need to make repairs. We mean to obliterate these Kiffians quickly."

Some of the Meshwesh agreed with Ramose, while others were not so sure. King Siti said, "We can wait them out. Starvation has a way of humbling a man."

Before we could discuss it further, we heard screams echoing through the tribe. Surely these Kiffians were not so foolish as to attack us with two legions of Egyptian soldiers present. In a rush, I left the tent to see what was happening. Faithful Ayn stood beside me, drew her sword and handed me her spear. Looking around I could see the people pointing in the direction of the city.

"Meshwesh dogs! Look what we have!"

I pushed toward the front of the gathering that faced the gates. A nasty monster of a man with long red hair stood on the parapet between the two center towers. He yelled at us in a language we did not understand. After his tirade had ended, he stood with his hands on his hips, two shield men on either side of him. The doors directly below him opened slowly, and a man rode out on a horse, dragging a half-naked woman with a chain about her neck. My heart melted in my chest. Pah!

"Sister!" I whispered. The Meshwesh gasped, and some even cried at seeing her. Ramose and my father came to my side. I stared in horror as the horseman dragged Pah around, ignoring her screams for help.

"Here is your queen, Meshwesh. See how we have defiled her? Advance any further and we will do more than that. Retreat now, or see her die!" Pah managed to stand, her red hair a matted swirl about her head. One breast was exposed, and she had blood all over her.

Ignoring Ramose's warning, I stepped out of the crowd and onto the sand alone. I waved the rest back. "Hold, men," I heard Ramose warn his archers who undoubtedly had the horseman in their sights. During this show, the parapet had filled with other warriors, including archers with flaming arrows. They wasted no time in shooting their fiery weapons at the ground before us, but I did not move.

I should have been afraid, but I felt no fear. Only anger. Deep, abiding anger. Pah shrieked as the savage jerked the cruel chain again. She began mumbling—no, praying—wildly, pleading with every deity she knew to deliver her. Pah's pleas were met with mocking laughter. "Silence now!" He reeled in her chain to pull her closer to him. She did not resist him and obediently quieted. The monster then turned his attention to me.

"Ah, another queen. Perhaps we should make a trade," he said leeringly. "This one is a bit used."

"What are your demands?" I yelled at him, ignoring my sister's pleading expression. I could not run to her now. We would both die. I had to stall for time, if only for Pah.

"Here is my demand—leave this valley, or we shall kill your queen," he said as he drew his dingy sword, "unless you have one to spare. And take these sons of Egyptian whores with you!"

"No! Do not kill her," I answered him. "We will do as you ask. What else do you want?"

I heard Ramose hiss behind me, but I ignored him. He wasn't in charge here. If I could keep the king talking, perhaps he would not kill my sister. I could tell he was not afraid of the Meshwesh or the Egyptians.

The stupid barbarian didn't seem to know what he wanted, so I prompted him. "Gold? Beer? What do you want? We will give it to you, only do not harm our mekhma."

"Yes, yes. Give us the gold and the beer, and then do not show yourself here again. Or we shall treat you even less hospitably than we did your sister."

"Who are you?" I demanded to know. "What is your name?"

"What does it matter?"

"I want to know who to ask for when I bring you your prizes."

"I am Gilme of the Kiffians. You can ask for me when you come. No tricks, or she dies and we hang her from the tower there." He pointed toward the city gates, but I did not bother to look.

"Very well, Gilme. I am Nefret. We will deliver your prizes to you by tomorrow morning. If you kill my sister or harm her further, we will never stop hunting you."

"Do you think that makes me afraid?" The men on the parapet jeered at me in their rude, rough language. As Gilme turned to grin at them I stole a look at my sister. Her eyes were wide with fear, and she shook her head slightly as if to say, "Please don't leave me." I said nothing and did not move a muscle. I could not appear weak in front of the brutes or my tribe, although there was nothing I wanted more than to cut her captor down. There were too many arrows pointed at us.

Gilme tugged on Pah's leash and dragged her back through the gate. She did not make a sound as she stumbled behind him. She never once turned to glance back.

A hush fell over the camp as they watched me return to them.

Ramose met me first, but he kept his mouth shut. I knew he did not approve of my negotiations, but he also had no idea what I had planned. I had never killed a man before and had no desire to do so until today. But if my ancestors gave me strength, I knew that I would kill Gilme. Slowly and with great pleasure.

The kings followed me and then gathered close, talking wildly about what punishment they wanted to administer to the Kiffian king. The sight of their mekhma in chains had lit a fire in them that no man would be able to extinguish, at least not without the shedding of blood.

"Listen! Start gathering your things. We will move the camp behind those hills there. I know it is farther from the water, but they will have to make do. Tell your people to draw what water they can now and then move quickly. Shasu!"

Amir appeared in front of me. "You must find a way into the city. Go west, behind Zerzura. Orba, you shall go with them. Help them find the Lightning Gate entrance."

Orba's eyes narrowed, and with a toothy grin he said, "I will not let you down, mekhma."

Ramose stepped forward. "Tell me what you have planned, as I am responsible for your safety. If you think I am going to allow you to walk through those gates and surrender yourself to the Kiffians, then you must be addle-brained. You cannot negotiate with these southerners. They know no language except cruelty, and they certainly will not negotiate with a woman—

even if she is a queen." The kings murmured against Ramose for the perceived slight. Even my less enthusiastic allies like Walida and Omel made no secret that they did not approve of the Egyptian's tone toward me.

The Shining Man must have been leading me in this because I then knew exactly what I had to do. I asked him in a calm, firm voice, "Have you ever heard the saying, 'The only Greek you can trust is a dead Greek'?"

"Yes, but I am surprised that you have." I ignored his scorn and met his level gaze. "Why do you ask?"

"I am a Greek. I am going to give Gilme a gift he will never forget."

Chapter Seven

Father of Queens—Semkah

As I woke I stifled a scream. Pain sliced through my arm like a hot dagger. I looked down and saw that I had no right arm. How could I experience such pain when the limb was gone, severed by a screaming beast of a man? I remembered the Kiffian who stole it from me and once again vowed that I would find him and repay him. Seeing the other bare arm with the snake twisting about the wrist, I thought wryly, "My destiny has been decided now. No need to struggle anymore."

I wiped the sweat from my face, and almost immediately the woman was by my side. Small and dark, she looked like a shadow in the dimness of my shelter. She barely spoke. I knew her name, but I had forgotten it—my mind felt thick, as if a blanket were wrapped around my memory. I struggled to piece together the most recent events. The tiny woman was constantly stirring pots, crushing roots, whispering over cups before she forced me to drink whatever brew she concocted.

Some days I felt strong, almost as strong as before. Other days I could barely escape the dream world; it was no longer a happy place to dwell. I could not remember the last time I had seen my wife in my dreams, when previously I would see her often even if only from a distance. I still dreamed of the cliffs where I first saw her, but she no longer waited for me there.

"Please, King Semkah. You must sit up and drink. This will clear your mind and ease the pain."

I pushed it away angrily, and the dark fluid sloshed on her hands. "Go away. Where is Farrah?" Then I remembered she was dead too and said, "Send me Orba."

"Orba is too busy to come wait on you. Remember? Your daughter Pah has been found, my King, and the mekhma has ordered us to move. You have to drink this so you can move without too much discomfort."

"I don't want your poisons," I whispered hoarsely. I struggled to sit up, and my tormentor did not help me.

She was not dissuaded. "You must drink this and we must leave. This is what the mekhma has ordered."

"Go away, woman." I leaned on my good arm and pushed myself up.

"You have forgotten my name again, haven't you?" She pursed her lips and without permission leaned toward me, lifted my eyelid and peered into it. "I see I have given you too much lophophora. I will not make that mistake again, but I cannot adjust this healing potion now. There is no time. Please drink. This morning's activities have stolen your strength."

In my sternest voice I said, "I have told you no. Now leave my tent. As far as I know I am still king. Go try your potions on someone else."

She snorted and stood. "Well, King, can you manage to stand up and get dressed? Whether you like it or not, we are short of healers in our camp. I am all you have. As I have said numerous times, we must go."

"I want to see my daughter."

"Then go see her." She stood with her hand on her hip, and her other hand still held the wooden cup. "I am not your prison guard. I am trying to help you, as Orba requested. I am sorry that I have not yet learned everything I need to know, but I shall."

I looked about me to see if there was something to lean on and spied the table not far away, but it wasn't close enough to be of help to me. The truth was I did need her help, or at least someone's help. Without a word, she set the cup down and stooped under my arm. She grabbed my hand and waited for me to stand.

"What is this lophophora you gave me?"

"It is a plant with white flowers. It is rare, but there is an abundance of it near here. The petals are worth more than gold. When you drink their essence, it numbs the mind to painful memories. I also rubbed an ointment made from the palm on your stump, and as you can see it has cleaned the incision beautifully although it stings for a while. The alora and alata herbs have a bitter taste, but they do help with the pain and heal the body."

"I want no more of this white flower. I want to keep my memories—all of them. Do you understand, Leela?"

"Yes," She did not move or offer to help me rise. When I finally got to my feet I thought I would fall, but she walked me the short distance to the table. I leaned against it, happy to depend on something besides her. I felt the blood rush to my head, but despite the discomfort it felt good to be upright again.

"Why am I so weak?" I growled at her. "This morning I was strong."

"Your strength will wane from time to time until the healing is complete. There is nothing I can do about that. Your arm was sliced with a poisonous blade. It did far more damage than you might imagine, and a weaker man would not have recovered. You are fortunate to be alive, my King. I suspect that if the gods did not desire it, you would not be here now. You will get stronger, I promise. You will not die."

"Don't talk to me about gods. I am not afraid to die." I puffed out my chest and grimaced at her. "Leela, that is your name," I remembered suddenly.

"Yes, that is my name."

"Tell my daughter I want to see her."

"I can't do that. She's with Ramose the Egyptian."

"Then tell my brother to attend me now."

She sighed in exasperation.

"What is it, Leela?"

"Drink this. It will give you strength and keep the pain away."

"And it will make me forget."

"Yes, it will."

"Dump it out. I will deal with the pain."

"Very well." She walked out of the tent and left me to tend to myself.

It was a challenge, but I didn't waste time. I stared a minute at my sword but left it behind. I could not use it, so why carry it? I chewed a piece of chula bread and gulped down some water for strength. This morning I had been strong, but now my hand shook and my head felt like a drunkard's, but I managed to get outside. Leela was right. The camp was about to move. Now I remembered Gilme, the Kiffian. And my daughter, chained and bruised by the hands of the savages. As I stepped outside, young women began packing my belongings, and I did not get in their way. "Where is Omel?" I asked one of them.

"There." She pointed to the east. I walked through the camp to find my brother. My daughter was alive. If I could help it, I would keep her that way.

"Omel! Where is Nefret?"

Omel turned in surprise at my voice. "Brother, you should not be here. You nearly fainted this morning. Take your rest."

"Don't talk to me of resting. Tell me about Pah. Who is this Gilme? Where is Nefret?"

Omel nodded to his men and said, "I will follow. Go now." He strapped on his sword and said to me, "Can you ride?"

The thought of having to pull myself up on a horse one-handed discouraged me from trying. "I am not sure."

He did not mock me but said, "Let us walk, then." We walked side by side up a slanted boulder that faced Zerzura. I could hardly believe we were here at the White City after all this time. It was heartbreaking to remember all the people who longed to see this place but never would. Farrah never ceased to believe that this day would come. But she would not be here to lead the triumphant procession into Zerzura; that is, if we did indeed breach the city's gates. Now my daughter was being held prisoner just beyond my reach. Knowing that she was so close but unreachable was torture, more torturous than knowing she would have to pay for her crimes—perhaps with her life. Still she was my daughter. I had to bring her back to us, no matter the consequences.

The city's gates were made of wood, but not any kind of wood I had ever seen. It had a reddish hue that seemed to glow with the fading sunlight. Even from this distance I could see that the planks were taller than any palm tree. The white stone walls flanked the doors neatly with no glimmer of light between them. Great iron rings hung from the front doors as if the giants themselves had bent them and placed them there.

"I don't see the Egyptians. Have they abandoned their task?" It could have been the remaining effects of the herbal brews Leela forced on me, but the back of my neck began to prickle. "Have they taken Nefret with them?"

"No. Why would they? What exactly has the mekhma promised Egypt, brother? Tell me the truth now. The gold or something else? Egypt would be a fool to take less than our mines after all this expense." He eyed me suspiciously as if I knew something he did not. That was Omel's way. He was untrustworthy and thought all other men so too.

"Aren't you always assuring us that Egypt's hands are bountiful? That Pharaoh wished for nothing more than to be a father to the Meshwesh? With my daughter at his court, he shall be. Why would you be so suspicious?

And you know that my daughter would never give away our treasures, Omel. Why must you be so distrusting?"

"What about my son? If Pah is there," he said, pointing to the gates, "then where is he?" He spat the question out. "Nefret should never have sent him away."

"We have all lost loved ones, Omel. If Alexio is truly dead, then I am sorry for it. He was a credit to our people, both brave and strong. But you should not bury him just yet. He may still return to us, and my daughter has said he is her most trusted adviser."

"And yet the mekhma chose to send him into the desert. Who advises her now? Ayn? Orba?"

Feeling weak I sat on a nearby rock but did not hesitate to meet his steely gaze. What was he implying? I barely recognized him anymore. The kohl around his eyes had begun to sweat, and he looked more like a demon than my brother.

He continued, "Can't you see this is the time for men to lead? How can we trust a girl to lead us in these difficult times? We need a strong leader, someone with experience."

"And yet you were willing to support Pah. Why is that, brother? Why do you so fear Nefret? Because you cannot control her as you could Pah? I will not make that mistake again."

Omel faced me, and I could see his hand twitch over his khopesh. For the first time, I believed Omel wanted to take my life and leave me dying in the sand. I stood and met his evil gaze with my own unflinching stare. If I was going to die at the hands of my brother, I would die standing, not cowering at his feet.

His hand began to slide the blade from its sheath, but then a strange thing happened. Stars began to shoot across the sky. They were close, so close that I could hear the sound of their powerful wings as they fell to the ground. Omel froze in his tracks and moved no closer to me. The sky lit brilliantly for a moment as one star fell into the desert.

"Semkah! There you are, my King! What a glorious sign! Did you see that? The stars are falling from Osiris' belt! This will certainly frighten our enemies, as they consider the Dancing Man their sigil. The gods are with us!" It was Orba. The small man climbed the rock and stood beside us, panting. "I have been searching for you everywhere. Nefret... excuse me. The mekhma is looking for you."

Omel rushed past him and left us standing alone on the rock. Orba watched him exit, and I sat on the rock again, the world spinning wildly. "I see the bear has a spike in his paw," Orba said quietly.

"If you had not arrived, I think he would have killed me."

"I believe you." He watched as another star flickered above us and sailed toward the mountains that stood behind Zerzura. "You should know that he has approached Ramose."

"What did he say to him?"

"That he should rule because Nefret was too young and inexperienced. He offered him the gold mines of the Meshwesh, but the general did not accept his kind offer."

I grinned at Orba. "You mean bribe. How do you know this, Wise One?"

"I heard them talking. Omel pleaded his case, but the general was unimpressed and assured your brother that he served Egypt only."

"I like this general more and more."

"I agree. Especially since Nefret will be leaving Zerzura soon."

"So you know?"

He bobbed his covered head. "I have seen her wearing the crown of Egypt. And when she does leave, there will be nothing to stop Omel from killing you. Of course if you had not sustained your injury, then none of this would be a question. But as it stands, my King..."

"I am well aware of the restrictions regarding my rule. Maimed kings are not effective."

"I do not believe this, but it is the tradition. However, there may be something we can do."

I sighed. "I am not such a man to believe that only I can rule. I am not my father or my brother. I will be happy to step aside when the time comes. But I am troubled that the Queen of Egypt has taken such an interest in my daughter. If what you say is true, that you have seen Nefret as queen, then that at least is something. I would still like to know how this queen intends to make that happen."

"Who can fathom the heart of a woman? It is unknowable, unfathomable and never predictable." I was surprised by his answer. I had never known Orba to marry or to love anyone. With uncharacteristic intensity he added, "It is not Omel that worries me. I have seen something. Something disturbing and evil."

"What do you mean?"

He shook his head as another star exploded above us. "We will talk more of this later, my King. Time is moving swiftly now, and your daughter needs you. With your brother lurking around with sword in hand, I do not think it is safe for you to be out alone. Let us get through tonight and perhaps tomorrow. Then we can talk about the future."

Slowly I climbed down the steep rock and walked with Orba back into the camp. "What plans have been made to rescue Pah?"

"I had no idea Nefret had learned so much about strategy from her father. Her mind is brilliant, and she shows nothing but confidence. At dawn Nefret is to approach the gate of the city with a wagon full of our treasures. She hopes to make an exchange for her sister. I cannot lie to you—I fear the worst is yet to come for Pah if we do not capture the city and rescue her."

"We have no evidence that the Kiffians will be anything but ruthless with her, and now Nefret will be walking into a trap—they will kill her too!"

Orba smiled grimly and said, "Ah, but it's not that easy to kill her, I think. If it were, she would be dead already. Someone is guiding her, I'm sure of that. No, my King. Her plan is much more complicated. You see, the Shasu are at the Lightning Gate. I have just returned from there. These Kiffians are so arrogant that they did not even bother to secure it! When the signal is given, the

Egyptians will appear to breach the main gate. At the same time, the Shasu will approach from the south."

I looked around the camp as we walked. I saw no Egyptians. "Where is Ramose? Where are the Egyptians?"

"Hidden in a place where Gilme would never think to look." Excitedly he began to share with me the details of the plan. I too was impressed with Nefret's ingenuity.

"And this was my daughter's idea?"

"Yes, it was."

"Then let us go see how I can serve her. I will not be left behind in this."

"No one doubts your courage, Semkah. But there is something the mekhma would ask of you."

"Whatever it is, you know I will help."

"This isn't an easy thing she is asking, but I encourage you to trust her."

Before I could question him further, another star, bright blue and burning, sailed across the sky. It was larger than the previous ones, and the size and nearness of it caused some alarm even in me. The people pointed and shouted at the sight. "What does this mean?"

Orba stared upwards and shouted, "It is a king's star! See how it falls?" The people murmured in wonder. "A king will fall soon. See where the star lands?" The crowd watched as the star plummeted behind Zerzura as the smaller one had earlier. "There is nothing to fear, Meshwesh, for the gods are on our side!"

The people clapped and hugged one another, and then went about their tasks. Everyone, from the youngest to the oldest, knew that our fate hung in the balance. But at least now the stars were aligned with us.

Maybe we would have a fighting chance.

Chapter Eight

The Unyielding Spiral—Nefret

It was good to see my father walking and talking. The fact that he was still in the land of the living was nothing less than a miracle. I wanted to run into his arms and wrap my own around his neck, but my people were watching my every move. We were facing the greatest challenge in our clan's history—I could do nothing that would hinder their courage. Most had no idea what I had planned, and the ones who did were not sure it would work. I heard rumors, thanks to Ayn and Orba, that my uncle and Astora were sowing seeds of discord as quickly as they could. Omel made no secret that he did not approve of my plan. The truth was, neither did I. But this was the only plan that presented itself to me, and I intended to execute it.

I helped load another bag onto the wagon. Traditionally we had no wagons in our camps, for we carried most things either on our camels or on our backs, but for this tactic we needed a wagon. The Egyptians had helped us assemble one quickly, and I hoped it would meet our needs. Or at least not fall apart before I made it to the gate. Ramose had left to put the finishing touches on the cart, and I could hardly wait to see it.

I faced my father and welcomed him with a smile. Now was the moment Orba and I had been waiting for.

"Father, won't you come and bless me?"

The people grew silent and waited to see what Semkah would do. Surprise crossed his face, but he did not deny me. Omel's eyes were riveted to us as my father began to bestow the tribe's blessing upon me. This was an ancient ritual, one that Pah had not enjoyed and one that I had not heard of until Orba described it to me. It was an old ritual that resonated with the elders of our tribe. They were the ones who needed to be convinced I could lead them.

Of course I wanted my father's blessing, especially on the eve of what might be my death, but this was for more than just me. Soon I would leave my Meshwesh people and return to Egypt. Someone would need to lead. Someone would need to guide. That had to be my father. At least until Pah recovered. I had seen her in the sand in front of Zerzura and knew that her mind had crumbled like a crushed flower. Who could blame her? What would I have done in that situation? I shivered at the thought. In fact, if it had not been for Pah's ruthlessness, it could have very well been me.

"Yes, I will bless you. Kneel now, daughter." I did as he asked, and he continued, "I bless you, Nefret hap Semkah, Meshwesh mekhma. I bless you with long life and good health. I bless you with all the blessings a father can bestow upon his daughter. Go with our prayers and good wishes." A tear slid down my face as my father's hand rested upon my head. I looked up into his handsome face, and he nodded down at me. "All will be well."

"I receive your blessing. Thank you, Father. Orba, Chief of the Council. Won't you come and bless me?" My father stepped back and allowed Orba to stand before me now. Although I knelt in the sand before the wise man, he barely stood taller than me.

"Nefret hap Semkah, I, Orba, Chief of the Council, bless you. We wrap you in protection and pray that our ancestors watch over you as you face our enemies. May the Unyielding Spiral of Life flow from your belly, renewing you mind, body and soul. May your bow arm be strong, and may you enjoy many days on this earth." His hands rested upon my head briefly, and then he stepped away from me. The gathering was quiet now, and the solemnity of this rare moment echoed through the tribe's consciousness.

"Omel, brother of my father. Won't you come and bless me?"

I kept my head down, but I heard surprised gasps echo through the crowd. Someone hissed quietly, but I did not turn to see who it was. I suspected Astora, and I knew Ayn would tell me later.

"Yes, I will bless you, niece." Omel stood before me and slid his shiny khopesh from its sheath. The sound of the metal rubbing against metal made my heart flutter, but still I did not look at him. I lowered my hands and placed them palms up in front of me.

Now was the moment. Now was the time. I could almost feel Omel's internal struggle. He would either surrender his sword or slice off my hands. I wondered which it would be. He paused for a moment, but I did not waver. I remained perfectly unmoving, my hands upraised, waiting to accept his sword—and his official submission to my reign. If he was to challenge me officially, now would be the moment.

"Nefret hap Semkah, I, Omel, Second King of the Meshwesh, bless you." His deep voice sounded like a growl, but he said the words, "As you accept this sword, may it strengthen you for tomorrow's fight and for all the battles you will face in the future. May victory never cease to be upon your reign as mekhma." He stepped back, and I clutched the sword by the hilt. I stood and raised it above my head, turning in circles so all could see it.

Then I cried out, "My people, my treasure, won't you bless me?"

With rapt faces, my tribe answered me with one voice. "Hafa-nu, mekhma! Hafa-nu!"

"I too bless you, Meshwesh! Hafa-nu! Pray for me this night, for tomorrow victory shall be ours. Finally we will walk into our city. We will take back our mekhma. Tomorrow, everything changes." They cheered, and I lowered my new sword as they rushed in to hug me and greet me. It was a moment I would never forget.

Once the crowd dissipated, only Father, Orba, Omel and Astora stayed behind. I could not help but notice that my uncle's wife had newly painted symbols on her face. Her fierce, painted eyes flashed at me, but she kept her thin lips clamped shut. My uncle did not speak. My accepting his sword had been a symbolic gesture; there was no reason to keep it, but I wanted to see if he would ask for it back. It was his father's sword, and I knew how he valued it. He stood waiting, but when I did not hand it back he stomped away with his wife in tow. I did not stop them or call them back.

With the hint of a smile on his face, my father said, "Orba says you have a task for me? How can I serve you, mekhma?"

"Father, never call me that. To you, let me always be daughter." He smiled broadly at this. It was good to see him smile. For the first time I noticed the strands of gray amongst his dark brown hair. "Yes, I do have a request. It is an unusual one, but please hear me out."

"Of course."

"We cannot talk here. Too many ears to hear." I cast an eye toward Astora, who constantly dogged my steps. Orba saw her too, and I could tell he was uncomfortable with her lingering. Stepping away from the crowd, I spoke to my father in a whisper. "After we have secured our victory, I cannot imagine it will be long before Ramose will want to return to Egypt. If that's the case, we may not have much time to decide on how to proceed. I cannot in good conscience leave you, Father, to fight Omel for the job. Tonight's ritual has bought us a little time, but it is only a temporary fix. My uncle will not stop until he has placed himself above all the Meshwesh. I have it on good authority that he approached the Egyptian general to ask for his help."

"Yes, I have heard that too. What did you have in mind?"

"Pah. She is still mekhma. But Father, she is not the same—she can't be the same as she was when she left."

"What do you mean?"

"You saw her in the sand at the end of the chain. She is out of her head. And even if she survives this, I cannot imagine she would be able to serve as mekhma. It would only be a matter of time before Omel seized control for himself."

Semkah ran his hands through his dirty hair and nodded. Looking at me with his sad eyes he said, "If she is as you say, then yes, we need to do something to protect her and our people."

Orba interrupted, "I mean no disrespect to either of you, but Pah has committed some serious crimes. She murdered twice, including Farrah, the Old One—these crimes cannot go unaddressed. The dead want their justice, and as the Chief of the Council, it is within my rights to demand it on their behalf. However, for the good of the people, for the benefit of the tribe, I am willing to forgo seeking justice until she is well."

Semkah shook his head. "How can you talk of justice now after all she's been through? Hasn't she suffered enough? We don't even know if she will live through this."

"I felt it only right to tell you the truth. What kind of counselor would I be to withhold this from you? I have seen Farrah and the child, and they demand justice."

I knew Orba was telling the truth, and I believed Pah was indeed guilty of the crimes she had been accused of, but my father was right. There must be some consideration for what punishment she had already suffered. Our ancestors had made sure Pah paid a price for her evil deeds. Yet, there were other things to consider besides revenge and justice. We weren't even sure that we could accomplish our plan.

I raised a hand. "Please, let us speak of something else at the moment. Farrah and my treasure, Paimu, will receive their justice, but we need to think about the more immediate danger, which is my uncle. He is maneuvering for something. Even though he has not received the blessing of Egypt yet, I am sure that will not be his last attempt. Here is my request, Father. I have asked Ramose to find Alexio and bring him back." I swallowed and felt the lump in my throat even as I said the words, "Pah needs a husband. A strong husband, a good husband, one who will not be influenced by Omel. I cannot think of anyone better than Alexio. I want you, Father, to bless his marriage to Pah. As her consort, he can lead our people until she is well again. At that time, these other matters can be determined. I fear if we do not take these drastic measures, if we do not find a strong consort for Pah, all will be lost. All of this will have been for nothing. I cannot say I am sad that Yuni died in the raid at Timia. He was a weak, lustful man. Pah was a fool to have married him, but now we must act."

My father lowered his voice. "I cannot tell you how surprised I am to hear this. You would ask Alexio to marry Pah? Do you know what you're asking?" He took my hand and looked into my eyes with concern.

"Yes, Father, I know what I'm asking. It hurts to even say the words, but this is the only way. As king, and you are king still, you can see it done. Alexio might resist you at first, but when he knows that this is my desire I'm sure he will obey. He would never betray me."

Then my father said what I did not think. "Aren't you betraying him? There is no doubt that he loves you, Nefret."

"I am mekhma. I will do what I have to do to make sure the Meshwesh are safe."

"Then if that is your will, let it be so."

"Yes, let it be so." Abruptly, I left them to their own counsel. The tears streamed down my face. Whatever Alexio and I had meant to one another, whatever promises and covenants we had made, I had now broken them. No—severed them with a cruel sword and chopped our love to pieces.

Things would never be the same. He was mine no more.

The camp was settling down now, and I found the makeshift tent that Ayn had installed for us. I had only a few hours to rest before we were to go to the doors of the city. Our camp had quieted, and so had the Kiffians'. Before the star shower there were sickening sounds coming from behind the walls of Zerzura. I could only imagine what kind of beastly things were happening. The sounds of screaming pierced the silence of the desert. Occasionally they would parade across the balcony, tormenting us in their crude language until the stars fell. Even though I served no god, I was grateful the sign had made them stop.

Ayn lay beside me. She smelled like sweat, but I could not complain. So did I. It seemed like forever since any of us had dived into the sweet waters of Timia. I know I should be excited to be so near Zerzura, our ancestral home, but I was not. I wanted to be anywhere but here.

"What are you thinking, Ayn?"

"I am thinking about how I will miss our people when we've gone."

Pushing my dirty hair from my face, I asked, "When we've gone?"

"You did not think I would let you leave by yourself, did you?"

I smiled at her but then pursed my lips. "Does this decision have anything to do with a certain Egyptian general?"

Even in the dark, I could tell that Ayn was uncomfortable with my question. She was not the kind of person who talked openly about her feelings—or her needs. I wondered which one he appealed to the most.

"If you are referring to Ramose, then no. It doesn't. I have no expectations of him. He has a wife, and he is an Egyptian. It would never work."

"I see."

"And what about you, Nefret? Although I think your plan is brilliant, I cannot believe you would willingly give Alexio to your sister. You have to know how she feels about him."

"I know, but we have no choice. It is Alexio or Omel. Omel's people will stir up Walida and others to make him king. He is a dangerous man."

She grunted and said, "You have no idea. Did you know the Egyptians call him Horemheb?"

"What does that mean?"

"Something to do with Horus. I don't know. These Egyptian ways are foreign to me. Apparently he is quite a regular figure at the Egyptian court."

"Is that what Ramose tells you?"

"No, I did not hear that from him."

With a sigh and a surge of concern I said, "Be careful, Ayn. Love is a treacherous mistress."

"I do not know that I love him, Nefret."

I smiled at her in the dark. "Yes, you do. Just be careful. And when we get to Egypt, trust no one." That was the advice I received from Queen Tiye herself. "We go to a dangerous place, Ayn. I fear that we will be at a disadvantage in many ways, and we will have no allies to guide us—unless you count my uncle. I am sure he will waste no time coming to the court, if for nothing else than to gloat over my situation."

It was her turn to laugh now. "That is what you are thinking about? In just a few hours you will drive to the gates of Zerzura and face the Kiffians, and you are worried about going to Egypt? Let us try to live through the morning. Then we will plan a strategy for survival at court," she said with a raw laugh as she tapped my arm playfully.

"I don't suppose there is a chance Ramose will change his mind and leave me here?" I asked hopefully.

"No, there is no chance. And if he heard you say that, he would lock you in chains now just to keep you from escaping." She whispered a warning, "So please do not speak those words in public. If Ramose does not return with you—safe and alive, I might add—he might as well fall on his own sword. He cannot disobey his queen. It would mean death for him, even if he does not truly care for her."

"He does not care for the Great Wife?"

"No, but he loves Pharaoh to no end. He is like a father to him."

"It sounds to me like Ramose trusts you a great deal, Ayn." I leaned on one arm and moved my messy hair behind my shoulder to better see her darkened face.

"I think he likes talking to me."

"And other things…" I said with a smile.

"I admit that I have never met a man like him before." We were silent for a moment after her confession.

"Be careful, Ayn. He is from another world, and we do not know how things will go."

"It is too late for that, Nefret."

Dread filled my stomach. "You said yourself you did not know if you loved him or not. What do you mean it is too late?"

Ayn's voice shook as she whispered, "I have his child in my belly. In our short time together I have given him something his wife never could—a child to carry his name. He will have his heart's desire—Ramose will finally have an immortal name. One that will last forever."

My skin crawled as she spoke. I did not know what to say to her, so I said nothing at all.

"Have I disappointed you, my mekhma?"

"No." I touched her arm and squeezed it. "Who am I to judge you, Ayn? Our tribe needs treasure. You know children are our greatest treasure." I tried to sound supportive, but I knew it would be much more complicated than that. How could I in good conscience take her to Egypt with me knowing she was with child? My eyes were sticky and my brain tired. I would not speak of this to her now. There would be other times to discuss her situation, and she seemed pleased with my answer.

"We had better rest if we can. Morning will be here soon. Hafa-nu, Nefret."

"Hafa-nu, my friend." In a few minutes, Ayn was snoring, probably dreaming about her Egyptian. My mind took me back to Alexio and our one night in the desert. It had not been that long ago, but it felt like a hundred seasons. His sweet smile filled my mind with sadness, and I imagined for a second that I could smell his warm and spicy scent. I could feel his strong arms around me as we lay together under the stars. It was a pleasant indulgence to dream about him now. However, if I was to survive, I would have to change the way I thought about him. I would have to put him out of my mind forever, for he would never be mine.

I suddenly hoped that I would die at the hands of the Kiffians. How much easier it would be if I did die! I would be gone, Pah could rule, and I would never have to miss Alexio again.

Because I could not immediately fall asleep, I let my mind wander like a wild thing. Eventually sleep did come, but it was fitful and full of faces I did not know.

Too soon, Ayn shook me until I was awake. A name fell off my lips, "Smenkhkare!"

Chapter Nine

Flames of Freedom—Ramose

The wagon lurched across the sand as I clung to the undercarriage. Beside me grinned Kafta—the crazy man loved schemes like this. He had not shaved since we left Thebes, and his beard and the sparse tufts growing around his head made him look like even more of a madman. As I clung to the pole with my arms and legs, I wondered if he was in fact mad. I could hardly believe that I, the great Ramose, General of Egypt, hung from a pole hidden at the bottom of a wagon driven by the Desert Queen. The Fates had a strange sense of humor.

When the girl shared her scheme, Kafta could hardly wait to mention using the barrels. He had done a tour with the Fourth Legion far to the north of Egypt when he first saw this battle technique employed. I could not comprehend the power he described until I saw it myself. When the liquid in the barrel ignited, it burst into flames. The explosion flung the dangerous liquid to great distances. It delivered a much more impressive display than an overheated kiln or a few fiery arrows. The barrels we would be using clunked near our heads, and I prayed silently to Amun that they would not explode and kill us all before we made it to the gate.

"Stick to the plan!" I reminded our driver.

"Shut up!" she yelled back as the wagon drove a few more feet before coming to a full stop.

"I like her," Kafta said, grinning at me through his gapped teeth. I rolled my eyes and listened carefully. Through the slit in the front of the wagon I could see that the gates were beginning to open. I could hear the sounds of metal, probably chains used to open and close the wooden doors. I heard the voices of the Kiffians as they jeered at the girl in the wagon. They were completely unaware that hundreds of Egyptians had been hiding in the sands most of the night, unmoving under their sand-covered wicker shields. I could not wait for the moment when this fact became apparent.

"Welcome, my queen!" A familiar voice, the voice of Gilme, called from above. I could see his position on the balcony through the slit in the boards. If only I had a bow and arrow I could kill the man now. But then hundreds of Kiffians would fall upon us and I would bring Egypt to war with these wild southerners. I was not sure what Queen Tiye had in mind for my charge, but I was certain it was not this.

"Please come in. We have been waiting for your promised gifts. My men are parched from a night of sporting." Gilme's rowdy men cheered loudly and laughed at their king's crude statement. "We want to taste this beer. You should pray that it does not taste like camel water. My men have particular tastes."

To her credit the girl did not hesitate. "I want to see my sister, Gilme! Bring her out now."

Without answering Gilme ordered the girl brought forward. I could hardly believe it, but she looked far worse than when we last saw her. Someone had cut off her hair, and she had fresh bruises on her face and naked torso. She was no longer in chains, but she had the look of someone who had been utterly defeated. I knew this look. I had caused it many times in the foreign leaders I conquered. It was common practice to humiliate a defeated king in front of his family, especially his wife. But the sight of this half-naked, broken girl stirred a rare sympathy in me. She did not look at us, nor did she appear to know where she was at all.

"Pah, come to me," Nefret called to her sister.

"She is not sticking to the plan," I complained to Kafta, who frowned back.

Gilme spat into the sand below him. "Nobody leaves here. You bring the wagon through the gate if you want to see your sister. She belongs to me now."

"That was not our deal, Gilme," Nefret growled back at him. Her words brought raucous laughter from the onlookers both on the balcony and in the open doors. I counted nearly thirty, but I was sure there were many more inside.

"I do not make deals with women. I do other things with them." That started another round of laughter from the Kiffians. "You need to learn your place."

The air crackled with tension. Gilme had done exactly as we expected, behaved shamefully and without honor. All the girl had to do was stand and raise her hand—that was the signal. What was she waiting for? I could hear the anger in her voice. She should have known there was no reasoning with a madman.

"This is your last chance, Kiffian king! Release my sister and leave the city! Do as I ask, and no one will get hurt! You have been warned!"

Sweat poured from my brow, and my arms and legs cramped as I held in place, clinging to the wooden pole. I did not take my gaze off of Kafta. Both of us realized that things were not going as planned and we needed to be prepared for anything now. I pulled my dagger from my tunic, ready to release the barrel at any moment.

"Do not refuse my hospitality, queen. Come now—you are wearing my patience thin." To someone below he ordered, "Bring the wench back into the city and close the gates until her sister decides to obey my commands."

I swore under my breath and whispered to her again, "Stick to the plan. Give the signal now!"

"Pah! Hafa yem taffa! Hafa yem taffa!" The Desert Queen yelled at her sister, and I felt the weight of the wagon shift as she rose to her feet. She let out a scream of anger as Kafta and I released the barrels and rolled out from under the wagon. In two seconds we were in the sand, rolling the barrels toward the gate as my warriors raised their sand-covered shields and stood screaming an intimidating war cry that startled the Kiffians. Arrows began to fly around us, and I dove for the half-nude girl standing before the gates. In a matter of moments, I had her in my arms and was running toward the wagon as the Kiffians began to return fire arrows wildly and yell in confusion. A flaming arrow whizzed past me.

"Get down now!" I screamed at Nefret as I ran to the back of the wagon with her sister. The explosion blew the barrels into oblivion and the flames burst up. Kafta's tactic had worked. The Kiffians, frightened and confused, could see my Egyptians now pouring into the gate. I glanced behind me and could see the Meshwesh approaching with unearthly speed on their horses as they streamed in across the desert. Nefret was suddenly beside me, reaching for her sister.

"Stay here!" I yelled at her, happy to deliver Pah into her hands. Releasing my sword from its sheath, I ran toward the gate. Bodies were already on the ground, and I was happy to see none of them were Egyptian.

My sword sliced flesh as I stormed through the gate. A great blond giant tried to withstand me, but he lasted only a moment. He wore no armor and succumbed to a single stab to his abdomen. I did not waste a stab to finish the job; he would die soon enough. I continued to fight my way toward the red-haired giant Gilme. He was my target—the only worthy opponent for Pharaoh's Great General. The Kiffians had no grace, no light hand with their weapons. It was sad, really, how easily they could be bested despite their size and tenacity. They carried evil-looking swords that they thrust at anything that moved.

Minutes later the Meshwesh made it through the gates, and I could see the Shasu running toward the melee from the other side of the city. Kiffians were fleeing before them. I ran up the stone stairs that I suspected would lead me to the tower and the balcony where Gilme had defied the Desert Queen. Despite the Kiffians' stupidity, it was not easy going—the balcony was full of warriors, both mine and the foreign king's. A bloody Kiffian cursed me in his guttural language, and I spun and swung at him. My opponent moved with surprising deftness, apparently more skilled than many of his comrades, but I did not relent. I swung the sword again, this time slicing his cheek and hand. With another howl he drove toward me recklessly. I mocked him with a laugh and moved easily out of his way as he fell on the stairs. In the blink of a hawk's eye, I slid my sword into his throat and grinned down at him as his miserable life left him.

I heard a woman's voice yelling threats beside me, and I turned to see Nefret engaged in single combat. She was in a deadly embrace with a young Kiffian who towered above her. I could see that he meant to overcome her with his reach and brute force. He had her hands clasped above her head and wore a lustful leer. As quick as lightning she brought her knee up into his groin and slammed her elbow into his face. He succumbed to the assault by doubling over, and the girl shoved her sword into his shoulder. The young man thumped to the ground like a bag of sand, and she stepped on his back as she ran up the stairs behind me.

"What are you doing here?" I demanded.

Her mouth was set in a grim smile. "You know why I am here." Ayn bounded up the stairs beside her. With a quick appraisal I could see Ayn did not have a scratch on her. Her long hair was plastered to her face with sweat, and her strong arms and legs were bare. Her sword gleamed red—proof that she had not idled the time away today.

"I am here, my mekhma."

Nefret glanced at her but did not turn her attention away from me. I growled in frustration. "I ordered you to stay with your sister. Why did you disobey my order?"

"Get out of my way, Egyptian." In reaction to her defiance, I reached toward her, but Ayn waved her blade at me threateningly. I could not hide my surprise.

"Do not get in my way, Ramose," Nefret warned me. I knew in an instant what the foolish girl had planned. She was going to challenge Gilme, and that meant she was going to die. I could not allow this—her death meant my death. If that had not been so, I would have happily allowed her to surrender her life to the Kiffian's sword.

In angry assent I nodded once and waved my hand as if to say, "Lead the way." Together the three of us cut into the now weakened line and drove toward our mutual target. Between administering blows I watched the women fight with surprising expertise. Nefret danced around her victims. She chose her offensive movements well and did not fail to deliver damage. To the untrained eye, Ayn's flurry of strikes might have seemed wild and frantic, but not to me. She planned her kills but enjoyed showing off. In that she was not wise. I watched as one of the Kiffians unleashed a fury of swings on her. Almost overwhelmed, she fell to one knee, her sword above her head as she pushed against his. In a burst of rage and a scream, the wild man pinned her to the ground, and a second Kiffian appeared tempted to join the fight or whatever they planned to do to Ayn. I flicked my dagger at him and pierced his right eye. He fell upon the other Kiffian, and Ayn quickly scrambled to her feet, stumbling away from them. Then with a showy swing, Ayn killed the man, grinned at me and ran after Nefret.

Many of the Kiffians were dead, but the few who were still fighting showed they were never going to surrender. Not in this life at least. At the center of the dwindling group was Gilme. He towered above his men, his beard wet with blood, and one of his ears had been nearly severed. The smells of war, blood, broken bone and burning fires filled the city of Zerzura.

"Kafta! Leave him!" I shouted to my second-in-command, who had every intention of claiming the giant for himself. In a few seconds, the six Kiffians remaining on the balcony surrounded the wounded leader. Breathing hard and savagely wounded, they looked at one another unsure what to do.

Finally, they fell to their knees, and two Kiffians immediately tossed down their swords in front of them. With a scream of anger, Gilme swung his sword, killing his own men.

He spat a vicious curse at them in his foreign language as the second man gagged and gurgled to his death. "You are not my son!" he declared to his writhing victim. Panting and weak, he faced us. He waved his sword with a blood-soaked hand and stared at me with burning hatred. "I will deal with you."

"I offer you no deals," Nefret answered him.

"I will never submit to you, girl."

"Yes, you will," she said confidently as she stepped toward him. Kafta looked to me for permission. In just a few steps, he could kill the defeated king or at the very least disarm him. I shook my head and watched Nefret. Gilme had lost much blood and wavered on his feet. She had enough skill to kill the man. Many in her tribe had gathered on the balcony to see their mekhma administer justice. If this helped her finish our mission, then who was I to stop her? Despite the queen's command, I would take matters into my own hands if she did not kill him quickly. I had my own life to consider.

Ayn stood beside me, her sword still drawn too. There was not much room to maneuver on the balcony, which was to Nefret's advantage. She was small, quick and largely undamaged by the battle.

Gilme glanced around him. All of his people, at least those on the balcony, had been mowed down. There was no one to help him. Looking past Nefret he called to me again, "You! I will yield to you!"

Nefret advanced toward him. She took two steps, and Gilme poked at her with his blade, but she ducked, stabbed at his chest and then swung out of the way. Surprised by her boldness, he yelled in anger but did not submit. I sensed someone else standing beside me and turned to see Semkah, Nefret's father, holding a dagger in his hand. Bloody from the fight, he yelled something to his daughter in their tribal language.

"Mey tanakha fama, mekhma Nefret!" In moments, the other Meshwesh—and there were now many on the steps, in the courtyard and outside the gate—repeated the phrase. I could see Horemheb bounding up the steps, and to my surprise he also had the cry on his lips.

"What are they saying, Ayn?"

Without taking her eyes off her queen she whispered to me, "My life for yours, Queen Nefret."

"What does that mean?"

Ayn's dark eyes watched me now. "These are covenant words, Ramose. It is a sacred promise to avenge the mekhma if she should perish. As she has offered her life for theirs, they do the same for her. These are sacred words you hear today."

The swords crashed, and Gilme used his hulking body to shove the Desert Queen away. But she rebounded and swung at him furiously with both hands on her sword. Gilme grunted as he fought her, and I could see his strength was waning now. As his arms fell back she had the opportunity to kill him but instead jabbed at his thigh, which began to bleed profusely. Gilme collapsed to the ground, and Nefret kicked his sword out of the way.

"Bring me my sister!" Nefret yelled at Ayn. The dark-haired warrior sped down the stairs, and the rest of us watched as the fallen king swore at the conquering queen. What was she doing?

Soon Ayn returned with Pah. Someone had tossed an ill-fitting tunic over the girl, but her eyes were empty except for the terror in them. She mumbled to herself, stopping only to scream if someone besides Ayn touched her or bumped into her. As the two cleared the stairs and stood on the balcony, I thought Pah would run or do something ridiculous like throw herself over the edge. But she froze, her attention on her sister, who stood over the dying giant of a man.

"Pah! Come now! Take your revenge, sister!" The crowd cleared a path for the girl. She did not move at first but soon began to walk and then run toward Gilme. Her father handed her his dagger as a scream of rage filled her lungs. Plunging her body forward, she buried the dagger into the man's heart. He did not fight his fate. We watched as the mad girl drove the dagger over and over into the corpse until, exhausted, she let the blade drop. She rose to her feet, her tunic now covered in blood. She backed away from Gilme and stared at her bloody hands. She took another step back and finally another until she neared the ledge. Yes! She was going to launch herself from the balcony gate.

"Ayn!" I shouted, as she was closer to the girl. Before Pah could finish her deed, Ayn and Semkah had grasped the girl away from the danger. She clung to her father and did not cause any more disruption. Soon the Meshwesh began to cheer for them both, though the cries for Nefret were greater, and the people began to celebrate their victory. Sliding my stained sword back into the sheath, I grasped Kafta's shoulder and congratulated him on his successful plan. Already my mind was moving toward the next phase. We would clean up the bodies and repair any damage to Zerzura, and then we would return to Thebes.

As if she read my mind Ayn caught my attention. She was a charred, bloody sight, but never before had I wanted a woman so much.

Surely she would be the death of me.

Chapter Ten

The Way Home—Nefret

The sun hung low like a dying ember in the sky when we dragged the last body from our city the following day. Such was the swiftness of the attack that none of our allied forces were killed and only a few Meshwesh were injured. Ramose congratulated me privately and informed me that the Egyptian army planned to leave tomorrow—then he and I would leave in the company of a small escort. I had only two days before I had to leave my people.

"So soon?"

His hands on his hips, Ramose replied, "It will not get any easier with the waiting, and the Queen grows impatient."

"You have heard from the Queen?" I asked apprehensively.

He waved his hand dismissively and replied, "I am familiar with the Queen's general disposition, and she is not likely to change her mind or tolerate excuses."

I understood his hidden message. *Do not ask for more time. It will not be given.* Desperation rose within me, but I fought back that wild beast with as much dignity as I could muster. It would do no good to ask Ramose to allow me to remain in Zerzura, and I would not demean myself to do so. The irony was, for all his Egyptian pride, Ramose was as helpless as I was. To the Great Wife, the general was a tool that served her just as any slave or servant did. Just as I did.

"Before I leave, I have a request."

"*Another* request?"

I pressed on, unabashed by his attitude, "It is customary for queens traveling to courts to have attendants, I am told. Is this true?" He nodded, and I continued, "This will be my second trip to Thebes, and I am anxious to proceed in a manner that will please Queen Tiye, my generous benefactor." I could see that my careful answer pleased him.

He flashed a white smile and looked relieved. "You may have attendants. Who did you have in mind? Besides Ayn."

"I wish to bring only two attendants, as we can hardly spare more than that. I will take Ayn and also my uncle." I tried not to smile at his surprise. And I silently prayed that he would acquiesce to my request without argument. I should have known better than to waste a good prayer on General Ramose.

"Now why would you want to do that?" Ramose sat on the edge of the heavy wooden table in my private chambers. Whoever had dwelt here while we were away had been generous enough to leave behind beautifully carved wooden and marble furniture. Surely that had not been the Kiffians.

Ayn lingered nearby, pretending she did not hear our discussion. She busied herself tidying my room, when in truth I owned hardly anything. I had noticed earlier that her things were in here as well, but I did not object. She had proved a faithful friend, even if I questioned her choice of lover. And I had to admit I was no expert on that. I could not make up my mind if I loved Alexio or hated him. I believed Astora less and less, and Ayn told me that she had never seen Pah and Alexio do more than flirt.

"I have never met your master, but I hear he is a shrewd man. He must be, to rule Egypt so well." I offered the flattery nervously, hoping it sounded natural. That got his attention, and he smiled again.

"Yes, he is the epitome of shrewdness." Suspicion grew in his voice, and he looked from me to Ayn, who did not meet his eyes.

"I can only imagine the cost of this campaign. I'm grateful for the Great Wife's attention, but I cannot imagine Queen Tiye would want to repeat this process. For whatever she thinks I am worth, I cannot imagine she would want to pay the price twice. Maybe you are not familiar with our agreement?"

"Enlighten me, please."

I kept my composure and proceeded with my lie. Another skill I had to learn, apparently. My soul cringed at the idea, but I had to think about my father, the children and all my people. I hoped the general did not know the truth about my conversation with the Queen. I was counting on it. "The Queen generously agreed to help me recapture my homeland and bring my people into a peaceful existence. With my uncle left behind, I am afraid the latter will not be true. Omel would surely sell my kinfolk, maybe even my father, as slaves to work in his mines. He is rich and growing richer by the day, but that is not enough for him. My uncle will not rest until he is the King of all the Meshwesh." At least part of what I said was true.

"Well, if you are not here, it seems to me that he would be the obvious choice as leader. If not him, who do you have in mind? For I can see you have thought about this. You are cleverer than I thought, Desert Queen."

Ignoring his last comment, I confessed, "I do have someone in mind. It is Alexio, Omel's son, who should rule." Ramose enjoyed a hearty laugh as he slapped his knee and then rose to pace the room as he rubbed his smooth chin with his tanned hand.

At least he has not said no outright. He is thinking about it, anyway.

Ayn was very near to him, and I could see he wanted to reach out and touch her, but he refrained. How could she bear this man? Yes, he had a handsome face and a strong body, but his condescending nature and rude manners would never suit me.

"How will that be any different? You said yourself he is Omel's son."

"Yes, but Alexio is loyal to me. And he is loyal to the tribe—all the tribes. As my sister's consort, he would keep the Meshwesh safe."

Ramose looked out the arched window of my chambers and watched the people below. The Meshwesh were tired but celebrating. Music rose from the streets, and the sounds of excitement filled the nearly empty city. Many families were camping in the streets instead of taking ownership of the empty houses. It would take some time for my people to become acclimated to this new way of living. I wished more than anything I could help them with this process. Now I knew they needed Alexio more than ever.

"I am sure your uncle would have some opposition to this. And if I allowed him to express his thoughts, he might even convince me to let him stay behind. I am not sure the throne would object."

Ayn finally spoke. "Mekhma, I have pledged to go with you, but if you find it better that I stay, as your father's or sister's protector, I shall. I know your heart is here." That got Ramose's attention.

Leaning his back against the window he quickly added, "In the interest of speeding up this process—I am anxious to be rid of this place—I will grant you your request. Horemheb, I mean Omel, shall return with us to Thebes."

"Thank you, General. Ayn? Will you please ask my uncle to come now? The sooner I give him the news, the better."

"Yes, mekhma. It will be done." She padded away quietly, Ramose looking after her as she departed. He made no secret of his desire for her. I wondered how that would change when we arrived in Thebes. I knew he was married, and so did Ayn. But perhaps in Egypt such things did not matter.

"Mekhma! Alexio has returned. He is on his way to see you," Biel stood panting in my doorway. The concepts of pausing at doorways and courteous knocks were a foreign thing to my people. Living in tents takes away the need for such things as privacy and courtesy. I did not scold him. He would learn the new ways soon enough from Alexio and my father.

"Thank the Shining Man for his protection!" I smiled and hugged the surprised Biel. I could not hide my happiness and had not thought to until I saw Ramose's face.

Biel did not notice the general's dark mood, or if he did, he did not seem to care. "Alexio is tired but anxious to see his mekhma. Did you know there were guards outside?" Finally sensing the tension in the room he added, "I am surprised to see the Egyptian here, mekhma. Is anything wrong?" Now Biel was scolding me for the perceived offense to Alexio. Did everyone know of our previous arrangement? Ramose looked like a tiger ready to pounce on the boy.

"All is well, Biel. Please wait outside. Let me speak to the general in private."

He shuffled his sandals momentarily but stepped outside as I asked, "Why are there guards outside my quarters? Am I to be kept a prisoner now? Couldn't I have escaped a hundred times already?"

"Yes, but now your lover has returned, Desert Queen."

I felt my face burn but did not rise to the general's bait. "I see you have been listening to camp gossip."

"Is it gossip?" He raised his hands to stop me from speaking. "I have no interest in knowing the secrets of a queen's heart, but I represent another interest: the interest of Egypt." He stepped toward me and was only a few inches from my face. He reached his tanned hand up and stroked my hair thoughtfully. When I did not melt under his seductive gaze or flinch away like an offended maid he said, "I cannot deliver you to Pharaoh's harem sullied, Nefret. He is not a man who likes to share anything."

"I am about to leave my home forever, General. Am I not allowed to say goodbye to the people I care about?"

"You may bid farewell to your father, sister...whomever you like."

"Just not Alexio? You know my intention is for him to marry my sister. Why is seeing him a restriction?"

"Do you think me a fool, Nefret? Marry your lover off to your addle-brained sister so that you can hope to one day return home to take her place? I assure you that if you were to do so, the full weight of Egypt would fall upon you and the Meshwesh. You belong to Queen Tiye now—Thebes is your home." As I stood open-mouthed, Ayn returned with my uncle. I was surprised to see Astora with them.

"Uncle," I greeted him, deliberately not acknowledging Astora. She was a snake—of that I was sure—and I would never again acknowledge her presence. "The general and I were just discussing my return to Thebes." Omel looked more of an Egyptian than Ramose did, with his wide gold collar and linen garments. I could see he had completely shed all signs of his Meshwesh heritage. And to think, he wanted to be the king of the clan!

He smiled broadly. "What a great honor this is for you and all of the Meshwesh! If only we had known the details of your new role at court...." He turned to Ramose, who did not deign to answer him. Neither did I. Even if I had known what I would be doing in Thebes, I would not have shared the information with him.

I smiled at him pleasantly. "Yes, an invitation to court is a high honor, as you have often told me yourself, Uncle. In fact, until recently I had no idea how popular you were with the Egyptians. I hear they have even given you an Egyptian name—Horemheb. Isn't that what we heard, Ayn?"

Ayn smiled at me. "Yes, mekhma. That is correct."

"Well, I have been privileged enough to receive a few kindnesses from Pharaoh's hand." He eyed Ramose with suspicion but asked him nothing. "I take pride in my name and in my Meshwesh heritage. I am doubly favored."

"In some ways, I have *you* to thank for this great privilege, Uncle. Without your connections and encouragement I would never have considered asking Egypt for help. Now, in the spirit of gratitude, I have decided that when I return to Egypt, you shall go with me. As my attendant, of course. We must represent our people with all proper decorum. Let me begin my career at court with the proper introductions. Who better to introduce me to the court than the great Horemheb?"

He began to stammer his refusal, but Ramose finally spoke up. "Surely your queen can rely on you, Horemheb?"

"I would never... that is to say...what about the tribe? I cannot just leave without..."

I touched his arm and said, "Leave the tribe to me, Uncle. I assure you I will not leave our people in disarray. Our absence will hardly be missed."

Smothering his surprise he replied, "Then I will do as you ask, mekhma." Astora stepped closer to him and he asked, "What about my wife? She is anxious to return to Thebes—she has family there. I assume she is to accompany her husband."

Still ignoring her, I spoke to Omel, "I have no need for another attendant, Uncle. I am afraid she will not return with us at this time. Perhaps later."

I saw Ayn smile behind Astora, but I kept my face blank. "Please prepare for the journey. We leave in two days."

He raised his hands in the sign of respect, then spun out on his oiled and sandaled feet, leaving only the smell of his cedar cologne. His wife lingered for a few seconds, long enough to cast a dangerous look in my direction, but she did not dare say a word in disagreement. I was still mekhma.

Feeling emboldened I said, "General, I expect you to remove those guards from my chamber doors. I am not planning an escape and have never given you reason to think I would. Whatever camp gossip you have heard, I assure you it is not true."

To my shock he did not argue with me. "Of course, Queen Nefret. I am at your service if you require anything." With a pleased smile he left Ayn and me alone. She reached out, took my hand and squeezed it.

"You handled him in fine fashion," she said, the admiration in her voice apparent.

"I don't think Ramose trusts me at all."

She laughed. "I was talking about your uncle. But no, Ramose trusts no one. Not even me."

I wanted to ask her if she had whispered to the general about Alexio and me. But if I was wrong, the slight would be unforgivable. She had never given me any reason not to trust her. Instead, I simply asked, "Ayn, I can trust you, can I not?"

"You know you can. Why do you ask me this?"

"I do not know. I am tired, Ayn. It is nothing. Please ask Biel to come see me. I am so hungry. Is there anything to eat? Maybe some bread? I can smell it, and it is making my stomach rumble."

With an uncertain smile she said, "I will bring you something. And I will get Biel for you."

The boy entered almost immediately, as if he had been listening at the open door. In a whisper I said, "Tell Alexio to meet me at the Lightning Gate. It will be well past dark, and I do not know how long it will take me to arrive. Please ask him to wait."

Biel nodded grimly and left me to myself. I sank down on a nearby chair, my hands shaking and my heart heavy. Whatever my fate, surely I could have this one night—one last meeting with Alexio? How unfair it would be to keep me from him for all eternity. No! It could not be! I would see him. I had to. And I would tell no one my plans. That way I would know for sure that no one had followed me.

As I waited for Ayn, I strolled around the massive room. I had not chosen this place; Ayn chose it for me. She said it was fit for a queen. The walls were white stone, smooth with joints so close together that you could not fit a hair between them. It was a magic place, Orba had whispered to me earlier before he left to search for a divine spring or pool for scrying. The doorways and windows were topped with arches, and there were interesting symbols and shapes carved into the surface of the stones above the doorways. I wondered what they might mean, but I did not have long to think about it. Ayn returned with a tray of food, and we ate in silence together.

Orba visited me that night and told me about my father's progress. I had thought to go see him, but the Wise One advised against it. "Semkah has exerted himself beyond what was necessary today, and I fear he needs even more time and care to fully recover. I asked Leela to give him a sleeping potion to help him rest. Naturally he constantly objects to her care, but in the end, he saw reason and is now resting. On the other matter," Orba said cautiously, mindful that Ayn was present, "I think that may prove more difficult than we first imagined. Your sister is not well, mekhma. I have had to move her from your father's room into her own just to keep him rested. Leela assures me that she can care for them both, but I fear Pah is beyond caring for." I swallowed the last piece of my bread and dusted the crumbs from my hands.

"What are you suggesting, Orba? That I put her down like a lame horse or camel?"

"Of course not. I wanted to make sure that you are aware of how sick she really is. She is out of her head and cannot carry on a conversation with another person, much less lead our people. The people will know that her spirit is struggling to keep her mind in one piece. Do you think they will stand by and welcome her once they see her walking around naked talking to herself?"

I no longer cared that Ayn heard our conversation. "This is why I want Alexio to become her consort. She will need his strength in these coming months. I have no doubt she will recover. Pah is strong—as she always has been. Besides, what alternatives do we have? Omel leaves for Thebes. And since my father is disqualified from reigning, there is no other choice. Surely you can see this. Unless the Council or its chief have decided another way around these rules?"

He patted my hand like I was a child and shook his head. "No, mekhma. There is no other way. You are right, of course, but I felt it my duty to share with you my concerns."

I squeezed his small, gnarled hand and returned a smile to him. "I am depending upon you, Orba. There is no one else. Do what you must to help, but do not kill Pah or harm her further. Please, I beg the Council for mercy."

He promised me nothing but said, "Perhaps you should see her. Maybe your presence will help her know she is safe. Also, I hear that Alexio has returned. When will you inform him of your request?"

"We will talk more about that later. I will see Pah soon. Go rest now, my friend, and leave these things to worry over tomorrow. That is when the real work begins. I'm counting on you."

The little man left, and Ayn and I finished tidying the room. This would be the first night we slept in a bed that was not on the ground. As we set about our task, I thought about Pah. With all my heart I wanted to see her, hold her, assure her that all would be well, but I could not forget Paimu. My treasure! How I missed her! I would see my sister, but not today. I was not ready to feel pity for her.

Instead, Ayn and I explored the many empty rooms around us and were amazed at the hawk carvings that stood outside the door of one large room, obviously a feasting area. Feeling tired but anxious to use every minute available to me, I walked the narrow streets beside my home and visited with my people. Many hugged me and reached their hands toward me. Many cried, "Hafa-nu, mekhma!" and I returned their greetings. Tears filled my eyes at the sight of the tired yet relieved faces of the Meshwesh. Tired we were, and many fewer than before, but we were home—back in Zerzura. To my surprise, many Egyptians patrolled the area, although most of them had camped outside the gate and I could hear the sounds of construction. Obviously they were attempting to repair the damage that had been done to the front gates. I had never seen such things as exploding barrels and fire bursting into the air. It was a powerful weapon, and now I could see why Egypt ruled the world. The things they knew far exceeded our own knowledge.

The sun had finally set as we made our way back to my chambers. Ayn hesitated outside the door, and I smiled at her knowingly. "I am sure I will be safe, Ayn. Go. See your general."

"This is our last night before we return to Thebes and to his wife. I do not know what the future holds. I want to treasure every moment."

"I understand that. Go. I'm going to bed." Ayn hugged me. It was a rare thing to receive a hug from the warrior. I accepted it, patting her on the back as she walked quickly down the street. As she turned the corner I took my chance. Now was the time to see Alexio! Ramose would be busy with Ayn and would never know. I turned the corner, deciding to take the long narrow backstreet that led to the Lightning Gate. I had no cloak, but the streets were almost empty. Most of the people had already settled in for the night and were unconcerned with one woman walking through the city. Still I stayed in the shadows as much as I could, silently cursing the bright moon that rose above me. I did not know the city well, but I headed north to where the Lightning Gate once stood. As I had promised, we had destroyed that gate today. There would be no entrance through that gate anymore. The stones had crumbled, and we would forever be safe and protected from the Nephal—and the Kiffians. I was panting as I scurried through the streets. I cleared the corner and nearly gasped when I saw an Egyptian soldier standing just a few feet away. He had not spotted me, so I quickly turned back and stood flush against the wall. I waited for him to walk by or walk away before I continued on my path.

After a short time, I poked my head around the corner to see that the soldier was now gone and the gate was in the distance. I did not see Alexio, but I hoped he had received my message and had found a place to wait until I could come to him. There were no buildings to hide beside now; there was nothing but open space from here on to the gate. I would have to run quickly to make it unspotted. I tossed my hair behind my shoulders, wishing again that I had a cloak to hide it. But there was no time for that now. I raced toward the gate only to hear a loud whistle echo through the courtyard.

"You! What are you doing here?" It was Ramose! Before I could answer him, he gripped my elbow and pulled me back to the edge of the courtyard. "You heard me. What are you doing here, Desert Queen?" I could not get free from his grip and stood frozen, unable to think or speak. Suddenly he shoved me against the wall and pressed his body against mine.

"Let me go!"

He stifled my cries by placing his mouth over mine and kissing me long and hard. I punched at his chest and pushed him as hard as I could, but he was like granite. I could not move him.

"You think to make a fool of me? I knew this was what you would do. Imagine, the great mekhma strolling through the streets like a common street—"

"Get off of me! I will scream, General, and you will have the Shasu upon you before you can think."

With a rough hand he grabbed my breasts and kissed my neck. "Scream all you like. Is this not what you wanted? Leave the boy alone, Desert Queen, or you will get him killed. I am a man, and I will keep your secret. I can please you."

Ramose kicked open the door beside us, and I could see his intentions. He would take me whether I said yea or nay. This was my last chance to reason with him. "And what about Ayn? What about your child? Do you care for no one?"

He froze just a few inches from my face. "What are you talking about?"

"Ayn carries your child. Finally, you will have your immortal name, General. But when I tell her what you've done to me…"

He pushed himself away and blinked at me in the dim light. "You lie."

"I do not. Ask her yourself. She has gone to see you." I straightened my clothing and wiped his kisses from my face.

His mouth opened and closed, but he said nothing for a long minute. He stared at me with his hawk eyes and then said, "Go home then, mekhma. But do not step outside your chamber door again. For if you do, I will not listen to your pleas for mercy."

Feeling numb I walked back to my temporary home, which was now my prison. I did not look over my shoulder or turn around for fear that Ramose was on my heels. I had no doubt he followed me at some length, and I believed his threat. For whatever reason, he would not allow me to see Alexio.

My heart felt like a brick in my chest as I walked up the steps and into my bed. Ayn did not return. After crying for hours and staring at the bright moon from my window I finally fell asleep.

Chapter Eleven

The New Daughter—Queen Tiye

I had no intention of letting the dust settle on her sandals before I made my purpose known to all. As I had learned from my husband, there was nothing like the element of surprise, especially when it came to outmaneuvering your enemies. Today was the day I presented my new daughter to the world. With only a moment's notice, my faithful steward summoned all the queens, the court and even my son to greet my new daughter. For a moment, I considered Sitamen and what this would mean for her, but only for a moment. I was sure she would misunderstand everything, such a sensitive child was she, but what choice did I have? My enemy, Tadukhipa, left me no choice! With my husband hovering between life and death, nothing could be left to chance. We had been foolish to invite Tadukhipa into our home—into our marriage—into our kingdom, and I refused to allow that mistake to continue through my son's reign. Hopefully, the steps I took today would knock that smug smile off her face.

I pushed the door open and walked into the Desert Queen's room unannounced. She stood in the midst of the room; a half dozen women, my cleverest servants, attended her. Immediately they all turned to face me, bowing their heads and shoulders in obedience. Even the girl had the sense to show respect to the Queen of Egypt. She was lovely, lovelier than I remembered. I had not seen her last night when she arrived, but my general made sure I was aware of her presence. Memre would serve her as her steward, hopefully to guide her in subjects like proper etiquette and basic traditions, things expected of her from the court of Thebes. This was such a complicated place, yet she was intelligent and I trusted that Memre would help her assimilate quickly. I had my eye on other candidates, but in beauty, intelligence and bravery, the Meshwesh girl had exceeded them all. I quietly congratulated myself as I walked around her, examining her hair and clothing.

My servants had obeyed me and had not shaved her gorgeous hair, nor had they yet put on her the dark wigs she would soon be expected to wear. Perhaps this was a mistake, but I thought not. Why not let the courts see she had been touched by the gods with her flaming red hair? Why not let them look upon her natural beauty before I took her into my household officially? Her hair was in two braids at her temples, which had been swept up and gathered at the back of her head in an elegant bow. Her startling green eyes were lined with kohl, making them even more intense, and on her lips was a touch of pink. My servants had dressed her in a blue gown that fit her youthful body perfectly, and the material... Ah, the material. It had been sent a week ago to the palace as a gift for Kiya from my husband, who remembered she had admired it during a recent trip with him. My servants had wrangled the delivery from hers and upon seeing it, I could think of no one better to wear it than Nefret. She appeared calm now, but I could only imagine what she was thinking.

"You," I commanded one of the servants whose name escaped me, "bring me those gold cuffs." The young woman quickly retrieved the jewelry and stood before me holding them neatly on a pillow. I removed the cuffs and placed them on Nefret's wrists. "That will do. Leave us."

As I stood close to the girl I could see that she was not quite as confident as I had imagined. She shivered visibly, but I did not ask her about her health. *She had better not get sick, not after the investment I made in her.* Fixing my gaze upon Huya, I said calmly, "You may also go. Wait outside." He did as he was asked, leaving me alone with the Desert Queen.

"How do you like your surroundings? Are your rooms pleasing? You may look at me."

She raised her head, and her eyes were like two pools of a green sea. I felt as if eternity were staring back at me. Yes, she was the one. The priestess had been right.

"Yes, Great Queen. My rooms are pleasing. Thank you for your generosity." I walked around her, examining her slender frame. She was taller than I, which was no surprise, but also taller than many women.

"My general tells me that you left behind some family. Tell me about them."

"My father is Semkah, the King of the Meshwesh. Or he was king until his injury."

"And your mother?"

She looked puzzled at my line of questioning but had enough sense not to ask me questions. "My mother was Kadeema, the Princess of Grecia."

"And where is she now?"

"No one knows, Great Queen. She disappeared into the desert, and no one has seen her since."

"Ah, so it is true. I have come to tell you the truth today, Nefret."

"The truth?"

"Yes. You were not the daughter of Kadeema but of Isis. It was she who gave birth to you and she who placed you in the desert." The look of surprise upon her face amused me, but only for a second. She needed to take my words to heart, remember them and say them.

"I do not understand, Great Queen. I do not know Isis or any other god or goddess. Once I thought I knew one, but now I am not sure."

I grabbed her by the elbows and pulled her close. We were only a breath away from one another. I could almost feel her heart pounding like a frightened rabbit in a trapper's net. I relished these moments far too much. Moments when I held absolute power over another life. But this power was also a grave responsibility.

"Do not say such things. I am the Queen of Egypt, the Great Wife of Amenhotep. I am Queen of the World and Priestess of Isis. I speak the truth, and you need to heed and obey. From this day forward, you are the daughter of Isis. Say it now!"

"I am the daughter of Isis."

Gripping her arms tighter I said again, "Say it louder!"

"I am the daughter of Isis!"

I dropped her arms and stepped back. I captured the dancer's pose—holding my left arm high and my right arm pointed behind me below my waist, I curved my hands in the shape of the holy symbol.

"Do as I do and say it again." I made the girl repeat the sentence over and over again until I was satisfied. "Do not think for yourself. Do not imagine you have permission to think for yourself. You do not. I do the thinking in this court. Still, you have a choice, a choice I did not have. You can live as a prisoner, or you can become a true Queen. Those are your choices. There is nothing else."

I left the Desert Queen alone to consider my words. It would not go well for her if she failed to follow my instructions. I was surprised to see my daughter Sitamen waiting for me outside the doors of the Desert Queen's room.

"Sitamen, why are you here?" I asked in a flat voice. She looked me up and down, examining the garb I wore as Priestess of Isis. She knew the importance of this event, yet I had told her nothing. Why should I? I was the Queen of Egypt and not beholden to any man or woman, even if that woman happened to be my own child. I looked up at her, remembering to soften my voice a bit. She had always been a tenderhearted child, and the condition had gotten worse as she got older. I blamed the Monkey for her latest flares for the dramatic. Before the arrival of the Hittite woman, Sitamen had obeyed every word and followed my instructions perfectly; now she had sold herself to Kiya in exchange for a few pleasant words and false compliments. The girl was a fool.

"So it is true, then. You are bringing this foreign queen into our court, into our family. Why?"

"And you have been putting your nose in places it does not belong, have you not, daughter? I do what pleases me. Why should I explain anything to you?" Fat tears hung in the girl's dark eyes. Sitamen had her father's heavy brows and few of her younger sisters' good looks, but she loved her brother as she loved no one else. While they were young, they were inseparable, but unfortunately for Sitamen, she would not be Amenhotep's true wife. He did not want her, or at least that was what he said now. Men were nothing if not changeable.

Before her emotions overtook her capacity for thinking, I had considered Sitamen intelligent. With a gasp of frustration, I walked past her, and she did the unthinkable—she touched the sovereign without being asked. She grabbed my arm just as I had held Nefret's. I froze and cast a look back, reminding her who was mistress of this kingdom. "How dare you place your hands upon me?"

"Mother, Great Wife of my father, it is I. Have you no care for me? Have you lost your mother's love for me? What have I done—why are you doing this? I am your daughter! You have daughters—why have another?" The servants backed away from us respectfully and silenced their whispering. Sitamen jutted out her angular chin and said, "Am I not a queen too? I should know what it is you are doing."

In a flash, I reached under her wig and grabbed a handful of her thick, coarse hair. I pulled her face to me as she yelped in pain. "I know well what kind of queen you are, daughter. Do you think I do not know where you spend your evenings? How dare you place yourself upon *my* level? How dare you think you are *my* equal! There is no one here who is my equal, not even you—fruit of my womb!" With a savage twist of my hand, I released her, taking with me a handful of her hair. The tears flowed freely down her face now, and she screamed in anger. She reached for the silver knife on the table, my knife, the one I used daily to slice into my pears.

Suddenly Huya appeared in the antechamber, but I raised a hand to him and stopped him in his tracks. Whether she knew it or not, having a blade this close to the Queen of Egypt was a capital offense. Thankfully she was not foolish enough to raise the blade against me. Instead, my daughter held the knife to her own throat.

I laughed. I knew and she knew that she would never have the courage to take her own life. Sitamen pushed the blade into her skin, and a stream of blood flowed down her pale neck. I stopped laughing, but my eyes never left hers. "Go ahead. Drain your life's blood and be done with it. At least then I will be free of your tears." I walked away from her, unwilling to give her one more moment of attention. I heard her weeping behind me, but I did not turn from my purpose. Huya was beside me, and I said to him, "Make sure she is in the court and in her proper place. I do not care if she is dead—I want her there."

"As you wish, my Queen." He scurried away to take care of his duties, and I stepped out on the dais to face the crowd. There were hundreds of faces perfectly painted and observantly staring back at me. In unison, they bowed, raising their hands in respect to me. Once, twice, three times. I held my head high in my fine silver gown, a snake crown upon my brow, a blue scarf wrapped around my shoulders. I accepted their greetings and cheers with dignity as I stood on the dais.

I did not sit, for no one sat before the arrival of the Pharaoh or his son. I could hear the crowd whispering—the excitement was growing. If what Sitamen said was true, the gossip had already spread through the courts. I wondered how many knew what I intended to do. There was a stir outside the court doors. My son had arrived, and the other queens were in their places in the lower court. I would not have to punish any of them today. The heavy doors opened, and I saw the face of my son, Amenhotep. He had been a friendly boy, sometimes friendlier than I preferred, but the people loved and respected their Pharaoh's son. Everyone, even the queens and I, bowed at his approach. As I rose, I studied him, remembering the boy I used to know. My mind was also filled with thoughts of another boy, my own precious Thutmose, victim of the schemes of the priest of Amun. They took one son, but they would not have another. Out of the corner of my eye I observed Kiya. She cast a lustful eye on Amenhotep, but she would never have him. In name only would she be his wife.

I turned my attention to Amenhotep. He towered above all those in his kingdom, even his father. He was built like a god. Today, he wore the double crown, reminding the people that he represented all, both Upper and Lower Egypt. In celebration of the special event, which he and only a few others knew about, his eyes were painted and he wore a fine necklace of turquoise and gold. A thoughtful gesture meant to please the Desert Queen. I wondered if she would notice.

Amenhotep climbed the steps of the dais and took his seat upon the throne of his father. It was an inspiring moment, even for me. As Great Wife to the current Pharaoh, it was my privilege to sit beside my son the Regent. He waved his hand respectfully to me, inviting me to take my place. I thanked him with a courteous nod and took my seat beside him. How thankful I was that he trusted me in this matter, and I would never forget it! I would have given my life for my son, just as I had been willing to give my life for Thutmose…if only I had known the danger he was in.

Huya waved his hand, and the court musicians began to play. The gathering whispered to one another, jostling to get a good position along the processional. Then a hush fell over the proceedings. The place was filled to capacity with curious onlookers. It seemed that even the paintings were peering down from the ceiling to see my new daughter. For the first time in a long time, my throne room seemed too small.

Horemheb and Nefret entered the outer court. Even from this distance I could see she made a striking figure. Slowly the pair walked down the aisle, and thankfully the girl did not gawk about her as if she were some farmhand. The people whispered, and she pretended not to hear them; as they approached, I sensed my son tensing. Yes, even he had an eye for beauty despite all of his religious ideas. Huya stood and performed a new song.

"In the name of Pharaoh Amenhotep, may he live forever, we welcome you, Horemheb, friend of Egypt."

As a dutiful and regular attendee of this court, Horemheb answered, matching Huya's cadence and tone. "It is with gratitude and a humble heart that I come here today into the court of my sovereign, Pharaoh Amenhotep, may he live forever."

"Friend of Egypt, what is your business here today?" Huya asked plainly with no song.

"Today I bring to court my niece the mekhma of the Meshwesh, Queen Nefret."

Amenhotep accepted her into his court by saying, "You are welcome in my court and in the court of my father, Queen Nefret." Respectfully the girl bowed her head slowly and showed deference to the greater monarch. I was pleased that she knew her place and did not need to be reminded to bow to her betters.

"Queen Nefret is the daughter of my brother Semkah and the Princess of Grecia, Kadeema."

"Stop!" I said firmly, shocking the crowd into silence. It was not customary for queens, even Great Queens, to interrupt a formal occasion. Still, this was why we were here today. "Is it not true that Kadeema, Princess of Grecia, the mother of Nefret, walked into the desert and disappeared?"

Surprised by my question, Horemheb stuttered and said, "Yes, Great Queen, that is true."

"There is no need to pretend any longer, no need to hide her identity, Horemheb, for I know the truth. She is safe now. I know who this Queen truly is." Horemheb wisely kept his mouth shut.

"Ever since I heard of this Queen, I knew the truth. And my historians have been hard at work to prove what I suspected." I leaned forward on my throne and looked down at the two of them. "This Kadeema, the beauty who disappeared in the desert, was not human.

She was Isis, the goddess. For a time, she made herself wife to Semkah, the King of the Meshwesh."

I enjoyed hearing the gasps in the gallery. Even the wide-eyed girl looked surprised by my words. With a small smile I asked Horemheb, "Do you know who I am?" Without waiting for an answer I continued, "I am Isis incarnate, her representative in this realm. And this girl is my daughter." Despite my warning, I heard Sitamen gasp. I would deal with her later. I turned my attention to the waiting crowd. "Do you believe me? Huya, come now. Read the lineage! Let all hear the truth and welcome my daughter! Finally I can reveal what has been hidden all these years."

"Tell us, Great Queen, what have you found?" Amenhotep's deep voice boomed across the gallery. "Let us hear this lineage so that we may also welcome the daughter of Isis."

As Huya began to read the lineage, the court became more excited. At the end of the reading they clapped their hands respectfully, accepting the lineage that had been written.

Amenhotep spoke again, "Today I welcome you, Neferneferuaten Nefertiti. And as the Great Queen gladly receives you into her family as her daughter, so I receive you as my sister. From this day forward you shall be treated with respect and shall be loved by all of Egypt." Huya walked toward Nefret, dismissing Horemheb with a wave of his hand. He led her to Amenhotep, who then took her hand and turned her to face the crowd. She smiled and nodded gracefully to the gathering.

"I shall call you Nefertiti, for truly a beautiful woman has come. Welcome, sister." Then Amenhotep did the unthinkable. He led her up the steps and invited her to stand beside him.

"My sister. You are most welcome here."

The crowd erupted in loud applause again, and many people shouted her new name joyfully. While Nefertiti enjoyed the waves of applause and admiration, I caught my enemy's eye. She did not nod in respect as was the tradition when the Great Wife looked at you or acknowledged you in any way. Queen Tadukhipa's face was a mask. A hard, dangerous mask. Amenhotep invited Nefertiti to stand beside him as he sat again upon his throne.

Just as directed, the court dancers and musicians entered and the celebration continued. All the while Nefertiti kept her composure just as if she had always been there. Music played loudly as the artists twirled and bent their lithe bodies to the tune in homage to the newly revealed daughter of Isis. When the dance was over I stood next to her and said, "Nefertiti, I recognize you as my daughter." In response Nefertiti made the sign of Isis, acknowledging publicly that she accepted the lineage that was read and accepted her place in the court of Thebes. I stared into her beautiful green eyes and gave her a small smile as we enjoyed the adulation pouring in from the court and beyond. The crowd had grown beyond the courts. Word had gotten out that the daughter of Isis had returned home to her mother and her court. It was a day of celebration.

I spotted a scarlet-robed courier pushing his way through the crowd, and my heart pounded. He traveled quickly to the throne and waited to be recognized by Huya. In our court, the wearing of scarlet indicated a very select order of trusted messengers. I held my breath as the courier came closer. Amenhotep waved the crowd quiet. "And what message do you bring?" The courier hesitated, but only for a moment.

"Alas, son of the great King Amenhotep. I bring the saddest news. Your father, King of Upper and Lower Egypt, heir of Ra, son of Ra, Amenhotep, ruler of deeds, beloved of Amun-Re, King of the gods and Lord of the Cataract, Giver of Life, has passed from this world's realm." The servant fell to his knees with his head bowed and waited on word from his sovereign. I gasped at the news. My husband and beloved was gone from me, never to be held in my arms again. I felt the weight of grief fall upon me, threatening to crush me before all who were gathered in this place. In a moment, what should have been the first day of a long celebration turned into an endless agony. Wailing and weeping broke out in the court. My son walked quickly through the silent court out of my chambers, probably to return to his father's palace. The court emptied in a matter of minutes. As the people left, I stared after them. Memre, my faithful servant, the one assigned to care for my new daughter, whisked the girl away. The once full court was empty now except for Kiya. She stood at the other end of the lower dais, and our eyes were fixed upon one another for the longest of moments. Both our hearts were broken, but I made no gesture of comfort to her. I'd had to share Amenhotep while he lived, but I would not do so in death. She offered none to me either. I spun on my heel and left her alone. At this very second, my beloved was preparing for his trip to the land of Osiris.

With wisdom, my servants moved out of my way, and I walked as quickly as I could into my chambers. I felt the warmth rising in my eyes—I had to find a place to let the tears flow. It was Amenhotep's last gift to me—to grieve all alone. What a cruel gift! No one could see my tears. No one could witness my heartbreak. This was the will of Pharaoh.

I remembered the day he said the words to me. The days and weeks after our son Thutmose disappeared into the sands never to be seen again, the palace had wept as one. Tears were flowing constantly, and as mine flowed my heart broke continually. Amenhotep, powerless to help me manage my grief and powerless to save our son, gave the command that no tears should ever be shed in my presence again so great was his love for me.

Oh, Amenhotep! Do not forget me, my love!

Chapter Twelve

The Garden of Life—Nefret

The court had grown quiet during the long mourning for Amenhotep. I was still a stranger in this strange place. Despite the warm welcome offered to me by Queen Tiye and some of her family, I knew this was not where I belonged. Every night I still dreamed of the desert. I dreamed of the ever shifting sand, the brown, smiling faces of the people I loved. I dreamed of my sister, laughing and confident and happy just to be with me. And of course, I dreamed of Alexio, and every morning I woke to find my eyes damp with tears. If it had not been for my constant companion, Ayn, I could not imagine how I would have survived these long weeks. Tomorrow would be the fortieth day—the end of the official time of mourning for the late Pharaoh. And from what Memre told me, what would follow would be a sustained period of celebration in honor of the new Pharaoh and son of the deceased king, also named Amenhotep. Since that first day here at the court following my return from Zerzura, I had seen neither Queen Tiye nor her son. On many occasions, however, I did see Sitamen and Kiya, neither of whom deigned to speak to me.

The court of Amenhotep was a lonely place, but I was used to loneliness. I was used to being counted out. If only I knew what game I was playing—or being forced to play. All I knew was what the Queen had told me. Memre was close-mouthed in regards to what the Great Wife had in mind for me, but I was beginning to see which way the wind blew.

During the quietness, I had the freedom to explore the Queen's palace complex. At the centermost part was Pharaoh's harem. A fine building with colorfully painted columns, many fountains and an abundance of children and women. Some women never left the small palace, but thankfully I was not one of these. They waited on the pleasure of the new pharaoh, and I imagined they thought of ways they could please him and bring themselves into his favor. I had ventured into that inner court only twice but found no friendly faces there. How lonely an existence that must be to wait day after day, week after week in hopes that your husband—or in this case, your royal lover—would visit you and show you some attention? How sad it would be to be one of those women. I prayed that this was not my fate.

Today, Ayn was gone on one of her many errands, and I suspected it involved her lover, Ramose. I never told Ayn of my confrontation with him or his threats to me. I could have pleaded my case to her and perhaps even convinced her to help me see Alexio one last time, but I could not bring myself to do that. Ayn was my friend, my only friend now, and I would do nothing to jeopardize that. For without her I would be truly alone. Horemheb, as I now called him, came to visit me once a week, sometimes bringing small trinkets and gifts and always asking for permission to return to Zerzura. I never granted it and never intended to. I supposed one day I would have to let him return and care for his family and see his wife but at the moment it was not in my heart to do so.

I strolled along an open portico lined with pretty pink and red flowers and enjoyed the sound of droning bees and the smell of citrus fruit. Yesterday, this place had been full of scribes and we had been forbidden to enter. Now the outside wall was painted colorfully and appeared as bright as anything I had ever seen. I had a genuine appreciation for the language of Egypt, much of which involved pictures of strange creatures and bold warriors. They were stories, I was told, and the Egyptians displayed them on almost every wall—even the ceilings of many rooms in the palace.

Over the past weeks, Memre had done her best to teach me some of the words and meanings of these strange symbols. Although I could speak the language as well as any, the writing was a challenge for me. However, I kept at it. I was a storyteller at heart and enjoyed the idea of telling stories with pictures. I stood along the end of the wall and stared up at the figures before me at the center of the action. I could see a tall, thin woman with an elaborate headdress. She wore a blue gown and golden sandals. She was surrounded by rays from the sun, and under her feet was a cartouche. Looking around I saw no one in the immediate area and set about trying to decipher what I saw for myself.

Nf…ger…

I heard the sound of tools working in the soil nearby. There were frequently gardeners in this area, but I had not seen any earlier. I was surprised to spot one now. Thinking to leave without getting him or myself into trouble, I turned to walk away, but the gardener called after me.

"You there." I turned and saw him wave at me. I waved back politely, not thinking to linger, but he said again, "You there. Do you need help?"

"No help. I was just looking."

Taking no refusals, the gardener ambled toward me, leaving his tool in the rich soil of the garden. He was tall and muscular, quite different looking than the eunuchs. "It is no bother. Do you like it?" He pointed to the wall.

So surprised was I that he would speak with me, I stammered a yes. "I do like it," I said, adding with a smile, "but I do not understand its meaning."

"I did not mean to eavesdrop, but I could tell you were struggling with some of the phrases here." He pointed to the cartouche and gave me a friendly smile, and for some reason I felt completely comfortable with him. How strange.

"I was that bad?"

"No, not at all. You see this phrase—the very first one? This is the sound." He pronounced the letters, and we pieced them together. I was surprised to hear that the name was Nefertiti.

"That is me!"

With a delighted smile he said, "Yes, Majesty."

I gazed up at the wall. "What does it say?"

"It says: Beloved sister of Amenhotep, Neferneferuaten, Beautiful of the Beauties of the Aten. This wall is a tribute to you—to your beauty. It is a declaration from Pharaoh to the world. He placed it here because he wanted all who visit this garden to see the beauty of his new sister, the loveliest of blooms."

I could not believe my ears. Why would Pharaoh care to do this? "I do not deserve such a gift. I hardly know what to say. Although I'm grateful, I do not understand Pharaoh's generosity."

The gardener nodded. "It must be difficult to be in a new place, to know very few people. The answer, however, is very simple. Pharaoh wanted to honor his mother's daughter. Just appreciate his gift. That is all that is required."

"I do. We do not have such beautiful art as this where I am from. I am sure my tribe would be astonished to see it." My comment elicited a laugh from the gardener.

"Is this place so different?"

"Oh, yes. Yes, it is. For example, if I were home I would not be spending my days walking gardens or learning this language."

"What would you be doing?"

"I would teach my treasures to climb trees, swim in the pool with my friends, listen to the traders tell their stories." I had not meant to sound so sad. "Forgive me for speaking so. I did not mean—"

"No apologies are necessary." Then he added, "Did you have a large family? Many brothers?"

"No, I had no brothers. I had a sister once." Strangely enough it, was not Pah I thought of but Paimu, the little girl who loved me and trusted me. Until I left her behind. How I missed her. How I wished she could be here with me. She would have loved to see this place. I turned my attention back to the colorful painting.

"Tell me, sir, what do these mean, what is this? It is a strange sign to me, so forgive my ignorance."

"That is the symbol of the Aten. It illuminates all who see it and appreciate it. As you can see here, the Aten has surrounded Pharaoh's new sister, enveloping her in its warmth and light."

I studied it, not knowing what to think or say. Impulsively I touched the stone, tracing the ray that streamed from my hand to the symbols beneath it. "Do your people worship the Aten, then?"

"All should, but only some do. What about your people?"

"There may be some who do. Like Egyptians, the Meshwesh are free to worship whomever they choose. Some worship their ancestors, others worship the gods of Egypt and others worship tribal deities like Ma'at. Here it seems kings and queens are gods. That is very strange to me."

"And whom do you worship, Nefertiti?"

I chewed my lip as I looked up into his bare face. It was strange to see someone who did not wear kohl or wear his skin oiled. "No one in particular. I once dreamed of someone I thought was a god. He was a Shining Man, and he came to me in my dream speaking very kindly. And when he left me, I felt at peace. I've never seen him with my eyes awake, and his visits in my dreams are very few. Sometimes I wonder if perhaps I did not imagine him."

"Tell me more about the Shining Man." I told him a few things that I saw in my dreams, and I was comforted to know I had someone to talk to besides Ayn. Ayn did not enjoy talking about spiritual things. Once she had worshiped our ancestors but no more.

Now here I was talking to a strange man in the garden about things I had not spoken to another living soul.

"I think you may be surprised with our new Pharaoh. He does not agree with many of the old ways and does not consider himself to be a god, although many around him want to bestow that honor upon him." In a soft, deep voice he added, "He worships the Aten—the Giver of Life."

"I must learn more about the Aten so I may speak to Pharaoh about the things he loves. If I ever see him again."

In a whisper he asked, "Would you like to see him again?"

"Yes, I would."

Someone was calling my name, and I turned to see who it was. I did not recognize the person but could see that he would not go away. I turned to say goodbye to the friendly gardener, but he was gone. I spun about and saw that even the gardener's tool had disappeared. I walked back to the steps to see what the man wanted.

"Yes, may I help you?"

"The Queen wishes to see you. Please follow me." I walked a long distance to a part of the palace I had never visited before. The eunuch opened the door, and to my surprise Queen Tiye was not in the room. Instead I saw the beautiful face of Tadukhipa, the one some people called Kiya. As we had not been formally introduced, I did not address her but merely stood in the doorway waiting for her instructions.

"Do not dawdle in the doorway, Desert Queen. Come in and take this bowl. Make sure my guests have been offered something to eat."

I did as she asked against my better judgment. The few times we had crossed paths in the past few weeks, I got the distinct impression that this woman did not like me and that her dislike was equal to my indifference. I could not understand why I had earned such a determined enemy, but I was often surprised by the women around me. Even my own sister.

Kiya's party was small. I saw Queen Tiye's daughter Sitamen lurking in the inner room, but she did not come out to greet me or speak to me. I carried the shallow bowl around the room dutifully and offered the selection of fruits to the women who attended Kiya's party. None accepted my offerings; in fact, none of them spoke to me. When I passed through the room with the bowl I dawdled around. Unsure what to do, I stood holding the bowl of fruit waiting for further instructions. Why in the world had she called me all the way here to serve her guests?

I had never been treated as a servant before, but she was a queen of Egypt. I looked at the steward, who pretended not to see me. I walked around the room again with the bowl, trying to stay out of the way. I had just decided to leave the unhappy company when Kiya made a strange sniffling sound.

"Well," Kiya said, sniffing the air as if she detected something foul, "what is this terrific smell? Camel dung? Is that the new scent from the exotic desert?"

Her game partner, Meritamon, shook the amber dice and studied the board before moving a marble game piece. Absently she answered, "Too earthy for me. What about you, Inhapi?"

The third woman did not speak but pretended to gag as she held her fingers over her nose and shook her head. The trio broke out into giggles. Anger whipped up within me like a desert wind. I let the silver bowl full of citrus fruits crash to the ground. It made a terrible clatter, and bright oranges bounced across the courtyard. Kiya sprang to her feet. "You pick that up, stupid!"

I stared at her with all the hatred I could muster. It was time to end this. I'd had enough of her snide comments. Very easily I could beat her to death with the bowl that lay at my feet.

"Never," I whispered ferociously. "I am not your slave!"

"Then I shall have you whipped like the goat that you are! How dare you defy me—I am the wife of Amenhotep! Pick up that tray, now!"

Before she could speak another word, Huya stepped out of the shadows from his hiding place along the outer wall. He was always lurking about. I had not noticed him before. He said nothing but merely stared at us. *Do not do what you are thinking*, his eyes warned me. I do not know what warning Kiya saw in his stare, but it held her anger at bay—at least for the moment.

The reality of my situation struck me as soundly as I imagined striking Kiya.

I was never leaving Egypt.

I had achieved the dream of all mekhmas. I had led the Meshwesh back to Zerzura, but there my story ended.

With my sister now ruling in my stead and Alexio at her side, there was nothing left for me to return to. I knew the truth of the matter—my star had fallen, my destiny had changed. I would never see Zerzura or any of my tribe again.

Yet despite it all, I lived. I remembered Queen Tiye's words to me before she left for Thebes, "You can live as a prisoner, or you can become a true Queen. Those are your choices. There is nothing else."

I would not live as a prisoner, nor would I be Kiya's fool. I made my decision.

I took a deep breath and picked up the tray from the floor. As I picked up each piece of fruit I made a resolution. I would condition my mind—I would never think of Alexio, Pah or my father or any of the other Meshwesh again. I would not cry over them or burn incense to any foreign gods for direction and favor.

I knew what I wanted—what I must do.

I would become queen of all Egypt. I would truly become Nefertiti.

Chapter Thirteen

Sisters—Nefret

Another week passed without a summons from Queen Tiye. Although I could feel the positioning of characters around the court, I had no way of determining the politics behind the various moves. Perhaps if I had taken more time to cultivate a relationship with my uncle, I might have consulted him or at least asked him for advice. But as he was not eager to be forthcoming with information, I was less eager to ask him for it.

One afternoon Ayn and I accepted an invitation to hear the musicians play at the Peacock Courtyard. It was so named for the abundance of peacock paintings on the floor and walls and for the wild birds that roamed there. I enjoyed staring at these bold blue animals. They were not friendly but were lovely to look upon. Sometimes they shed their feathers, and I had taken to collecting them for decorations in my stark rooms.

Ayn and I took a seat on one of the empty benches and listened to the tambourines and lutes play fine tunes. The music was different from that of the Meshwesh. It was more melodic, more organized. One man stood before the gathering of seven musicians and raised his hands as if he were magically summoning the notes from the instruments. It was an amazing sight. To my surprise, Queen Tadukhipa joined the gathering and took a seat beside me on a nearby bench. We clapped politely between songs, and during one interim she whispered to me, "They play beautifully, do they not?"

"Yes, they do." This was a complete turnaround from the woman who had mocked me just a few days before. Once the music had ended and the musicians were leaving the court, Kiya turned to me with a sad smile. "Nefertiti. Sister. Please forgive my behavior the other day. Since the death of my husband it has been very difficult to be kind to anyone. You did not deserve such ill treatment."

"I do forgive you." I said the words as I was expected to, but my heart warned me that something was amiss. A shadow passed behind me, and I shivered. Sitamen had entered the courtyard. Upon seeing me, she gave a sound of disgust. Without a word, the girl exited as quickly as she had entered. Kiya laughed and called after her, but she did not answer.

Kiya said, "You must understand Sitamen's position. The poor girl wants to please her mother. To learn that the Queen has a new daughter…well, that was quite a shock to her."

"I deeply regret causing Sitamen any heartache, as she is the Queen's true daughter."

"Perhaps you two can be sisters," she said in a whisper.

"I have a sister," I answered defensively. Ayn poked me in the side, and I immediately regretted giving Kiya any information about myself.

"Yes, I heard. Pah-shep-sut, that is your sister's name?"

"No, just Pah."

"My mistake. I want to show my sincere apologies for my behavior by holding a banquet in your honor and perhaps introduce you, if I may, to my circle of friends. It has been my belief that it is always good to have more friends than enemies. I know a great many people would like to get to know you better. Would you be my guest this evening?"

"Unless the Great Wife needs me, yes, I will be your guest. Thank you, Queen Tadukhipa." In a rush, she rose from the bench and smoothed her gown. With a perfectly lovely smile she looked down upon me and gave me a courteous nod.

"Very well, my steward will come to collect you at dusk. Of course, you should come alone. There will be plenty of people willing to serve you, Nefertiti."

She left me staring after her, and Ayn poked me in the side. "Do not trust her, Nefret."

"Ayn!" I whispered to her viciously. "Be careful what you call me. You know the law here. My name is Nefertiti."

She stared at me suspiciously. "Have you forgotten who you are, mekhma? Who you truly are?"

Frustrated, I snapped, "What can I do but survive, Ayn? What can either of us do?"

"So you have given up, then?"

"What are you talking about? There is no rescue party. I am never going home, and as long as you serve me, neither are you." I hated the sad look that crossed her face, and I immediately apologized. "You must regret accompanying me. Egypt has not been a happy place for either of us, but at least you have your Egyptian."

She seemed offended by my comment, although I had meant nothing by it. "What does that mean, Nefret?"

"I told you to call me Nefertiti."

"I will call you whatever I like." Her hand rubbed her belly protectively. She did that more often lately as her belly had begun to swell. I secretly wondered what the protocol would be when the steward discovered that Ayn was pregnant. I had seen a few women swollen with child during my stay at the Queen's palace, but it was not an everyday occasion. Would they send her away? I prayed not, but I could not imagine that I would be allowed to keep a baby in my chambers. We had never spoken of it, but perhaps we needed to.

"Ayn, please. I did not mean to upset you." I reached toward her, and she squeezed my hand.

"Forgive me. I do not know why I feel so... so... so much of everything right now."

"Come walk with me," I whispered as we strolled along one of the private walkways in the Peacock Courtyard. I shooed one of the territorial birds away. I slid my arm through hers and leaned my head on her shoulder for a moment. "What does Ramose say?"

"I know he is pleased to have a child. I do not see him as often as I once did, but as you know he is not a man to share his thoughts with me or with any woman. Sometimes I think he loves me, and other times I do not. I do not know what I will do, Nefret—I mean, Nefertiti."

"You can go home, Ayn. Home to Zerzura. I release you from your vow to me. Go home and raise your child in peace in our city."

"Where he will be hated because of his father? I would rather stay here, if that is possible. I do not know how much longer I can hide the child, though. Memre watches me like a hawk."

"Memre watches us both like a hawk. In fact, she looks like one." At that we both had a good laugh.

"Yes, indeed." Ayn smiled at me, and we walked some more in silence. "What has become of us, mekhma? Did you ever imagine you would be here? I never did."

"No, I cannot say that I ever imagined this. I wish I could hear something from home. Some word about what is happening. Horemheb is punishing me, I think. He refuses to tell me anything, and yet I know he knows exactly what is going on."

"Did you know that he seduced your sister?"

I froze on the path and released her arm. "What? Omel and Pah? Why would she let him touch her? He is a repulsive snake—not to mention our uncle."

"He filled her head with promises. He promised to make her mekhma, and he was not alone in his choice."

I gulped. "Father?"

"Oh no. Your father was not involved in any of that. He was willing to let the Council choose, but he had no idea Omel was involved in the process. Omel even convinced Farrah that you were too weak to lead. I think she never trusted him."

"Yet she went along with the decision to make Pah the mekhma."

"Yes, but that was mostly because Pah had the sight. She could see in the fire *and* the water. Above all things, except for returning to Zerzura, Farrah wanted to see into that realm again."

"Why have you never told me this?" The sun blazed above us, and Ayn was visibly sweating. I saw my friend the gardener working in a corner and nodded to him as we passed. I hoped he would be around later so we could talk more. I took Ayn by the arm again and led her into the coolness of the palace toward our chambers.

"Why would I have told you? They were wrong. You were—no you *are* the mekhma by right. If not for the Kiffians, I think you would still be at home."

I considered her words for a moment and said, "No. Without the Egyptians we would never have found our home again. To think they knew the way and we did not! Fate is a cruel mistress."

Later that evening, Kiya's steward came to retrieve me. I had no idea what to wear for the evening meal, but at Memre's suggestion, I wore a plain white gown with a jade green necklace. I think Ayn was relieved to be freed from the prospect of an evening with Kiya. I wished I had been in her position, but if I was going to manage to survive in this court I needed to find an ally or two. At the very least I needed to know what my enemy was thinking. And Kiya was my enemy. I had no illusions about that.

I followed the pudgy man down the lighted hallways until I stood once again outside Queen Tadukhipa's chambers.

"Here she is. Our guest of honor. Welcome, Nefertiti." The queen clapped her hands politely and urged her dinner guests to do so as well. There were many more people than I had expected, but I smiled politely and thanked her for her invitation. In a great show of friendliness she kissed my cheeks and complimented me on my dress. She herself was dressed in a pink gown embellished along the hem with gold coins that tinkled as she moved. Her feet were bare, but she wore anklets and her arms were full of gold bracelets. Upon her head was a slender circlet in the appearance of a rising snake. As always, she wore a long black wig. The queen led me to a seat at her table, and I sat beside her. "Sitamen, our guest has arrived. Please, come and greet her."

The smallish woman approached me with her eyes downcast and her hands clasped before her. For some reason the motion reminded me of Pah. "Nefertiti, I am Sitamen. I'm very happy to meet you. Would you like some wine?" The crowd applauded at the kind words and gesture. Kiya thrust an empty cup into my hand, and Sitamen poured the wine with a demure smile.

"Everyone, please raise your glasses in honor of our new sister, Nefertiti. Let us welcome her to Thebes. Please introduce yourselves." The gathering obediently lifted their glasses to me. One by one they visited my seat and told me their names, and I quickly gave up trying to remember them all. I sipped the wine until it was gone and placed the empty golden cup before me on the table. After the formalities were complete, musicians began to play immediately, and I recognized the tunes from the concert earlier.

Sitamen sat beside me on a pink cushion. "Here come the dancers!" She clapped her hands ecstatically. "How I love these new dancers. Wherever did you find such talent, Tadukhipa?"

"My steward, of course. He has a keen eye for talent." Kiya raised her glass again and prompted me to do the same. Still trying to navigate these strange social events,

I felt compelled to comply. I picked up the now full cup and took another sip. Yes, I could taste the herbs in this wine—some type of spices. It would be easy to lose yourself in these cups.

"Tell me, sister," Sitamen whispered in my ear, "do you dance? What do Meshwesh dances look like? Are they anything as fine as these?" With her knees pulled up to her chest and her arms wrapped around them, she studied me as she plucked some grapes from a bowl.

"We dance on special occasions, like at weddings."

"Oh, are you naked when you dance?"

I could not hide my shock at her question and laughed nervously. "No, we do not dance naked. I never have."

"That is a shame. I hear it is remarkably freeing. My mother—I mean, our mother—often tells me about her experiences with the Amazon women. She says they dance naked around a big fire before they go to war."

"That must be very difficult during the heat of the summer."

"Are you mocking me?" Sitamen's voice rose as her heavy-browed eyes narrowed.

"No, I am not. I am sorry you would think so."

She pursed her lips and said, "Who are you, Nefertiti? Really?"

"I am as you see me. There is no mystery here." Sitamen took another sip of her wine and raised her glass to me. As it seemed to be the custom, I took another sip myself but silently pledged to drink no more. I had abstained from eating anything before I arrived, as I had believed there would be food served at this banquet. And already my head felt light.

"If that is the case, then I want to hear all about you. Tell me about your sister, your true sister. Was she very much like you? And if so, why did my mother claim you and not her? If I am to believe that you are truly the daughter of Isis, would not your sister also be?"

I blinked at her. My head felt as if it were in a fog. How could a few sips of wine make me feel so woozy? "Why ask me these questions? Why not ask your mother?"

Someone at the other end of the table called to Sitamen, and with a final indignant look she left my company to visit her friend.

Kiya said, "She is very bitter, but she is also a sweet girl. Give her time to acclimate herself to the idea of having a sister."

"She already has two sisters, from what I understand."

"Yes, but they are very young and do not share her interests." She sipped her wine again and poured more in my cup, but I did not pick mine up this time. When a platter of bread arrived, I snatched a piece of it off and wolfed it down without a care for what I looked like. She laughed, and the sound was pretty but empty. "I had no idea you were so hungry. Here, have some of these." She passed me a bowl of dates, but my stomach was not cooperating with me. I felt sick. I rose to my feet quickly, which caused me to feel faint. My stomach did somersaults, and I had a growing suspicion that someone might have poisoned me. At the very least, my stomach was rebelling against the flavor of this Egyptian wine.

"Excuse me," I muttered as I walked out of the dining room and onto the balcony. Perhaps some air would do me good. I stood clinging to the side, hoping the world would stop spinning around me.

As I held onto the balcony railing and waited for the reeling to stop, I saw a man walking up the steps. He was simply dressed in a white skirt and a neatly folded headdress. His hands were behind his back as if he were in deep conversation with himself. His body shone with oils, and around his neck rested a wide gold necklace. As he walked toward me I recognized him. This was my friend the gardener. He did not see me at first until I hissed to get his attention. I did not want him to get into trouble. Men were not supposed to be here, especially after dark, unless they were eunuchs. Although I had no firsthand knowledge of my friend's status, I assumed he was not.

"You cannot be here. Queen Tadukhipa is just inside. Go now."

He paused and laughed as he stood on the top step. "What?"

"You cannot be here. There are no men here, especially gardeners. Now go away before someone sees you."

He laughed again. The curtain separating the dining room and the balcony opened, and the queen stepped out with the evil gold cup in her hand.

"Nefertiti. Drink this. It will clear your head." Seeing my visitor, she froze and bowed to him immediately.

"I can explain," I said quickly, trying not to vomit in the queen's presence.

She did not wait for my explanation. "Pharaoh! I did not know you were here. You honor me with your presence."

My heart thundered. "Pharaoh? What are you talking about?" I pushed my hair out of my face to get a better look. *This could not be true, could it?* As a wave of dizziness struck me, I clutched the low stone wall tighter.

"Tadukhipa. Is my new sister drunk? I will take that," he said, still amused. He reached for the cup, but the queen drew her hand back, sloshing the wine on the clean white stone beneath her.

"No, Majesty. Let me get you a fresh cup. You need not drink after us." Her eyes were wide, and I could see she had caught her breath. It was as I suspected!

Not used to being refused, he said, "Give me the cup, Kiya." With faux confidence, and trying not to react to the insult, she passed him the drink. I watched as he sniffed the contents and looked at her suspiciously. He held it to his lips, and she stiffened. "Is that juniper I smell? No, I cannot drink juniper. Here, you drink it." He passed it back to the queen, and she did as he commanded. Her face became unreadable as she stood holding the empty cup. He waited for a few seconds and then said to me, "Come, Nefertiti. Walk with me." My head and stomach were still revolting against me, but I managed to place my hand upon his and together we left the wretched party.

"I think she poisoned me."

"No. If she had, you would be dead already. However, I would not put it past her to make you sick. Most people do get sick on juniper wine when they first drink it. I suppose if you were to believe my mother, Tadukhipa might do that. Just to embarrass you before her court."

I nodded, thankful that I would not die, no matter how miserable I felt. "I feel sick, Majesty. I am sorry."

"The best way to reverse the effects of juniper wine is to walk."

After a brief pause I accepted his hand again and did my best to keep up with him. "You are Amenhotep. I thought you were a gardener."

"And that is what I wanted you to think. I had to know you for myself, Nefertiti. A man cannot always rely solely upon his mother's word. However, she was not wrong. And it is true that I enjoy the act of planting and bringing forth a harvest from the ground, but I do not share that knowledge with many people."

"Wait. Your mother was not wrong about what?"

"Wrong about you. You are both brave and lovely."

I did not understand completely what he was talking about, for my head was still foggy and my mind screamed that I was walking with the Pharaoh of Egypt. I had expected him to be completely different. Pharaohs were cruel—they were distant kings, untouchable by their people or by anyone—but Amenhotep was not so. He was real and available and a friend. On his arm I glided down the last of the steps, and we walked out into an area of the palace I had not yet explored. My stomach still swirled in turmoil, but I did not slow my pace.

"What is this place? I have never been here before."

"I would imagine not. It is the Great Wife's private gardens. She rarely comes here anymore since my father left for the life beyond."

The dark trees gave off a fragrance I had never smelled before. I breathed it in and found it helped clear my mind somewhat.

"That is frankincense you smell. It is the scent of kings. Did you know that?"

I shook my head and smiled as best I could.

There were white stones under our feet, and birds chirped at us as they settled down for the night. The sun had set, but there was still much light in the walled gardens. "Why did you let me believe you were a gardener?"

"As I said, I wanted to know who you were." Finally, we sat together on a bench under a cluster of palms. He removed his headdress, and I could see close-cropped black hair. And although he did not wear as much kohl as some, he was very much an Egyptian. "I have not stopped thinking about our conversation, about this Shining Man you saw. I have to tell you the truth. I have seen him too."

I could not hide my surprise. "Truly? When? What did he say?"

"He told me that he was the Giver of Life, that he was in everything, that he was the breath we breathe, the life within us. He promised me that he would help me rule my kingdom and that he would guide me throughout my life."

"If you trusted him," I added, remembering what the Shining Man had told me.

"Yes," he said with a surprised laugh. He rose to his feet and took me by the hands. Looking into my face tenderly, more tenderly than any man ever had, he asked, "Will you come with me?"

"Where are you going?"

"I am going on a spiritual journey. I want to find the home of the Shining Man, as you call him. I call him the Aten. I want to find his home and then build him a temple worthy of him. There are no temples to the Aten here; the gods of Amun and Ra own this city. I dream of a new home, a new Egypt. I want all my people, even my slaves, to experience the love and peace that the Shining Man brings. The great Aten deserves the praise of all Egypt. Come with me…" and then he added in a low voice, "and be my queen."

Perhaps it was the wine or his words. Maybe it was the Shining Man. I do not know. I do know that was the night I fell in love with Amenhotep. That was the night everything changed.

In my mind's eye I remembered my dream, the dream of running through a darkened city of stone, a child running behind me.

Smenkhkare!

I would never forget the child's eyes—the eyes of my son. And I was seeing them now. They were the eyes of Amenhotep.

Still under the influence of the juniper wine I whispered, "I have seen my future, and it is you." With a happy smile he put his hands under my chin and tilted my face to him. He kissed me, and the kiss was a promise. A promise of a friend who would walk beside me on this unusual path, the path determined by the Shining Man.

A few hours ago he had been the gardener. Now I would spend my life with him. For him I would abandon all others.

I was now the Queen of Egypt.

Chapter Fourteen

Blue Scarab—Ayn

Nefret had departed the city with Pharaoh, leaving me behind without an explanation. No matter to me—I was burning for Ramose. When I was not crying. Motherhood had weakened my emotions to the point I could not trust myself to speak to anyone for fear that I would snarl at them like a beast or weep at the friendliest word.

I would be lying if I did not acknowledge that I was hurt by Nefret's slight, but then again I was only a servant now. Perhaps I should go home. At least there I would be free.

When Nefret returned to her chambers after Kiya's banquet she was quiet—quieter than usual, and she spent a lot of time staring out the window at the stars. There were no longing looks toward home. Normally she would have told me everything, but that night she remained mute.

The following day, before she departed, I went to the kitchens to find food for the two of us. The palace was abuzz with the news—Nefertiti would be queen. I returned with a bowl of food, some fresh fruit, bread and cheese and barely got through the door before I asked her if the rumors were true. I need not have bothered. Servants began pouring into her chambers, sent by Pharaoh himself. Some carried fine clothing, others jeweled chests containing more jewels. This was all the proof I needed. With excitement Nefret—no, Nefertiti—welcomed them and opened all her treasures.

Sullenly I watched it all. Naturally my mind went to Ramose. It had become more difficult to see him. When I visited the training grounds now he was never there, or if he was, he was too busy to come to the gate to let me in. Yesterday I went to the practice field but was turned away.

Today I was determined to see him—my situation was becoming more desperate, and if Ramose did not agree to help me, then I would have to find somewhere else to take my seclusion. The last thing I wanted to do was return to my tribe with an Egyptian child. I knew I would not be welcome there despite Nefret's recommendations or influence. Children were cruel, even Meshwesh children. No, my son, for I was sure it would be a son, needed to be with his father, the General of Egypt. I had to make Ramose understand— I had to show him how important it was. In the flurry of activity in Nefertiti's chamber, I left easily enough. I wandered around until she left and then I turned toward Ramose's barrack house where I worked during the day training young soldiers and developing plans for Pharaoh's campaigns, which Ramose complained were too few of late.

As I turned into the brick building, a familiar soldier spotted me and disappeared into the inner offices. *So much for surprising Ramose.* I waited patiently outside the barracks—it was not wise for a woman to walk in unattended even though the men there knew who I was. I was pregnant, but I was still strong and could handle myself if necessary. At least that is what I told myself. As I hoped, Ramose walked out to greet me. Before he could send me away I said, "I must see you. If I don't, I will have to leave."

He took me by the elbow, led me into his office and ordered his men to leave. They followed his orders, and only a few cast me sidelong looks. A few months ago they would have been beaten for even looking in my direction. That was not so anymore. I kept my head held high and did not show them the shame they hoped to see on my face. I was a Meshwesh warrior, not some camp follower. I loved Ramose—yes, this was love. I had given myself to him freely, and I felt no shame in it.

Was he going to help me, or should I leave? That was the question. I was not afraid of him, for I knew he would never harm me, but he could be cruel with his words. And as my heart had been quite tender of late, I did not want to engage in a painful discourse. I need not have worried because his lips were upon mine. His right hand kneaded my tender breast, and his left hand went around my waist. I kissed him back, welcoming the warmth and taste of his lips. My desire for him rose as it always did, but my mind would not allow me to surrender without knowing first what he intended.

"Listen to me first." I resisted his embrace, and my lover did not hold me. "What about my son? From what I am told, I cannot stay in the palace in this condition. I will have to leave, Ramose—leave with your child—unless you help me."

"What are you asking me?"

"Do you want me to stay?"

Ramose was never a man who enjoyed talking about his feelings. That I knew. Yet I had to know. I was not so good a lover that I could read his mind. He would have to talk to me.

"I think I have a solution if you will hear me out."

"Very well."

"You know that my wife and I cannot have children. That is plain to me now, but perhaps the gods found another way to bring my son to me."

"Yes, they have," I said with a smile. Feeling a surge of love for him, I reached for his hand and placed it on my belly. "See? There he is, moving and kicking already. A strong boy—just like his father."

Ramose's dark eyes displayed his emotions perfectly. He did want this child—more than I had first thought. I began to feel hopeful again. He had not cast me off—not yet!

Gently he rubbed my shoulders and said to me in a serious tone, "Ayn, you must give the child to me. My wife and I can raise him as our own. She is willing to do this—I have spoken to her already, although it was difficult to do so. Inhapi understands the ways of the world, and she is willing to accept my son, but..."

I could hardly believe my ears. "But what?"

"After today, I cannot see you again. What was between us is no more. That is the price. I am sure you agree it will be worth it."

I stepped back, nearly falling over a pile of empty beer pots. "What? Give up my son? To Inhapi?"

"Stop before you harm yourself," he said gently as he reached for me. "I am not asking you anything unreasonable. It is done all the time here. The gods chose you to be the mother of my son, but surely you knew that I would never put away Inhapi. Nor can I deny her this request. She has been a good and patient wife to me."

"Good and patient? I would not use those words to describe her. Nor would you, until this day. How can you ask this of me? Do you not know that I love you? I have given you my body and been your lover these many months. Why tell me this now?"

"Calm yourself. We never spoke of love, you and I. We were two warriors who battered against each other and found some comfort in one another's arms. I admit that I care for you—care for our son—but this can never be anything more than that."

Never would I have imagined such words would fall from his lips!

I felt as if I were being smothered. I had to get away—out of his presence. I walked toward the door, but Ramose blocked me. "I have to know your answer, Ayn. If you do not agree to this, you will have nowhere to go. Inhapi will see to it that you are turned out of the palace. She has powerful friends, my wife."

"And you? The mighty General of Egypt? You are powerless to stop her? That is what you want me to believe? Curious turn of events, Ramose. I wish I had known from the beginning how weak you truly are." To my utter surprise, the man I had loved so fully slapped me savagely. I fell to the ground immediately, and blood filled my mouth.

I did not stay down for long. "You hit me again—touch me again—and I will kill you." He did not try to stop me again, nor did he strike me. I left the barracks and practically ran back to the palace. The many faces I encountered were a blur to me. They were strangers, and as I ran realization dawned on me. I needed to go home. I could not stay here; there was nothing for me in Egypt. I must leave, even if it meant losing myself in the desert.

I did not enter the front gates of the palace. I chose the side entrance, showing my face only to the palace guard stationed there. He let me pass, although he did look curious at my appearance. I clamped my mouth with my hand to prevent the blood from leaking out. By the time I made it to Nefret's chambers I had a mouthful of blood, which I promptly spit into a nearby bowl. Then the tears came freely. I had no worries about snooping servants; since the new queen was absent, there was no one to spy on me. I could hardly believe my sad situation. I had always prided myself on being wiser than most women, stronger, more independent, and here I was in the same situation that stupid farm girls found themselves in every day.

When I pledged myself to Nefret I had intended it to be for my whole life, but now I had to put my son first. I had to leave Thebes. For where, I did not know. All I had to do now was wait until she returned. I could not in good conscience leave her without speaking to her. I must thank her for all the things she had done for me. She trusted me when no one else would—indeed, I did not deserve such favor. I had been a fool for Pah, and now I was Ramose's fool as well. I refused to be Inhapi's fool too!

I decided I would stay in Nefret's chambers and steer clear of everyone until she returned. It could not be forever, could it? If she did tarry too long, I would simply have to leave. Ramose had made it clear that Inhapi would seek revenge if I did not agree to her terms.

I lay on my bed, the tears gone. My mind swam with possibilities. I dreamed of my mother's arms holding me, swinging me up into the air as she told me to fly, cradling me when I burned with fever. *Oh, Mother...I miss you. How I miss your arms!* In my dreams, I buried deep in them and lay my head upon her chest. I could hear her heart beating, feel the warmth of her skin, smell the scent of the garlic and onions from her kitchen.

It was as if I felt her arms now. I shook myself and found a face hovering over me. Inhapi!

She shook me awake, and I snatched myself from her grip.

"Get up, whore! Get up now!"

"What? What are you doing here? Who let you in?"

Without hesitation she climbed over my bed and came after me with something evil and shiny flashing in her hands.

"I gave you a chance. I gave you a chance. If you do not willingly give me my child, I will cut it out of you."

"You are a madwoman, Inhapi! Leave now!" I threw the bowl of blood at her. It stained her dress and clattered on the floor.

"Go ahead and scream. I hope someone does come. You are to be turned out, Meshwesh whore. Your Desert Queen will not help you now. And the true queen here, Tadukhipa, agrees with me. You and your red-haired friend have to go."

I surveyed the area. My weapons were in the closet, and I could easily kill Inhapi, even though she did not know it. If she did not cease her attack, she would find out. "I warn you, Inhapi. Do not test me. I have been fighting much longer than you, and I will hurt you."

"You can try, Ayn, but you may not find me so easy to hurt. I am Ramose's wife, remember? I know about hurt." She circled around the room. There was a small table nearby with a flat platter on it.

Grabbing the platter with both hands, I warned her again. "Leave now or you will regret it."

"I could say the same to you. If you manage to make it out of this room alive, you had better run as fast as you can because you will never be free. Do you think you are the first, girl? No, you are not. And you will not be the last."

"Then why are you here? Should you not be talking with your husband?"

She waved the knife at me stupidly, and I smoothly ducked her. I felt less worry now about the immediate danger, having seen firsthand her amateur style. She had no fighting skills, except those involving poison and gossip. I put the platter down and waited for her to swing again. She did, and I grabbed her wrist easily, shook it and watched the knife clatter to the ground. "Let go of me! Keep your filthy hands off me."

Feeling tired and frustrated, I whispered to her as I held her close to me. "Why? Your husband did not mind my filthy hands at all." With a vicious scream she slammed her head into mine and punched me in the throat. Crumpling to the ground, gasping for air, I stared up at her in complete surprise. Then she fell on me, and the knife appeared again. She raised her hand above her head and brought it down as if I were an animal sacrifice and she an evil priestess. Grabbing her hands desperately as I wheezed for breath, I twisted the knife and in a clumsy move, she fell on the blade. It slid into her easily, and she collapsed beside me.

"Oh gods! Inhapi!" I stood over her as her mouth moved like a fish needing water, just as mine had a moment ago. I watched in horror as the woman stopped breathing and her blood seeped out on to the floor. Now I had to go. I could not wait for Nefret. There was no time to pack or plan. I grabbed Nefret's cloak and the blue scarab that Ramose had given me some time ago. I looked back sorrowfully at what I had done. It had been an accident, but who would believe that? The general's lover—a foreigner—killed his wife.

Death would be coming for me, with all of Egypt.

Oh, Ramose! How could you do this to me? How could you betray me? Now you will hate me, and we will forever be separated. If not for our child I would have thrown myself off the balcony, but I could not. I had to live. If only for him.

Chapter Fifteen

The Aten—Nefret

When the litter stopped at the dock, I could scarcely believe my eyes as I peeked out from behind the sheer curtain. I had heard of boats and had seen men fish from small flat ones at the Biyat Oasis once, but this was altogether different. This boat was larger than any I could have imagined, and already the sounds of celebration had begun even though Amenhotep and I had only just arrived. A billowing white canvas was staked into the ground, and we were invited to embark under it. Unsure how to behave, I followed Amenhotep's example. I kept the smile from my lips and trained my face to remain unaffected by it all. It was a difficult task.

As soon as I stepped on board my stomach lurched, but I hoped the unsettled feeling would subside soon. If I could survive juniper wine, I could survive anything.

The boat seemed more like a floating palace than anything else. The flat, wide bottom must have helped keep the thing afloat, and for the first few minutes I had a secret fear that we would all sink. More billowing fabric hung from the sides, protecting the occupants from the bright Egyptian sun. It floated and popped in the breeze that blew in from the river. The cedar floors were sturdy, and I could see carpeted floors just inside the doorway. Stepping inside after my attendant, I marveled at the blue walls bursting with images of crocodiles, birds and a myriad of other fascinating animals that were unknown to me. We walked through the open room and through another door. Inside was a bedroom with sumptuous carpets, flickering gold decorations and the faint smoke of incense. I swallowed nervously and looked about the room.

It appeared I would share my chambers with Amenhotep, but that did not surprise me. I was to be his queen now.

"Your bed is made, lady. Food is here too. Would you like me to pour you a bath?"

"Maybe later. What is your name?"

"Menmet, lady." She cast her eyes down, but I could see a small smile on her face. Menmet had an interesting accent, one I had never heard before. She was small, not as petite as Queen Tiye but much shorter than I. And she wore very few clothes. Her gown was sheer, so sheer that I could see her dark nipples through the fabric. Egypt was a strange place. I hoped I would not be expected to walk around so. I blushed and turned my attention to my surroundings.

I walked to an open window and watched the crowd that had gathered at the dock. A few well-wishers had followed us, but now there were many, including a large number of priests. I knew these were the priests of Amun because they wore leopard skins. No others, besides Pharaoh, could wear those. They stared at us, whispering amongst themselves.

"Menmet. What are they doing here?" I might as well ask someone who might know the reason for this gathering. I counted two dozen priests now, and the numbers were growing.

"Lady, those are the priests of Amun. They come to protest this journey."

I was shocked. "Why? Because of me?"

"Oh no, lady," Menmet's narrow eyes widened that I would ask such a thing. "Not because of you, Beautiful One." She whispered, "The priests of Amun do not like the Aten, and they think the Pharaoh is wrong for taking this journey to honor the god. They say to us that there is no real god but Amun, and the priests of the Aten say the opposite." She stared back at them and stuck out her tongue.

"What about you, Menmet? Whom do you worship?"

She sighed as if it were the most difficult question in the world. "Whoever I am with, I worship their god. It is much more peaceful that way. How do I know who is right? I leave those things to the priests."

"Oh, do not say that, Menmet. You can worship whomever you like. Do not let someone else dictate to you who to worship. I do not think Pharaoh would wish that."

She shyly pretended to examine her feet but said nothing.

"What is it?"

"You can say this, lady. You are the daughter of Isis. I am the daughter of Heb and Shupset." Her tone was not disrespectful; it was matter-of-fact. She believed every word. I knew I was no such thing, except to please Queen Tiye.

"Nefertiti!" Amenhotep came into my chambers and surveyed the arrangements. "Do you like your room?"

"Yes, Majesty. I do."

"Good. Very good." He stood with his hands on his hips, his smile brimming with confidence. "Rest now, and I will come to you before sunset. Together we will watch the Aten leave the sky."

I bowed my head in agreement, and he left. I had guessed wrong. He did not plan to share my room. This boat was very big indeed to house us all. "I am not sleepy, Menmet. Let us arrange the things." I could feel the boat move and said, "Ooh…" I sat down quickly.

"Poor lady. Have you never ridden on a boat before?"

"No, I am afraid not."

"It will pass soon. Let me get you some wine."

I made a face and asked, "It is not juniper wine, is it?"

She crinkled her nose, and for a moment she reminded me of Paimu. "I would never serve you that, lady. No, this is good wine from a land far to the north. They call it…what is it? I cannot remember, but I will be right back."

I sat in the chair and clutched the sides as I waited for Menmet to return. I drank what she brought me, and she was right. There was nothing as sweet and delicious as this northern wine. After Menmet led the other women in arranging the room, they lay down in various places. I lay on my cool bed, the wine helping me to sleep soundly. I woke with Menmet talking in a low voice.

"Lady, Pharaoh has come. Rise now, lady."

I climbed out of the bed, sipped some water and exited the chambers under the watchful eyes of my twelve ladies. Amenhotep waited for me along with another man I had never met before. I did not get an introduction before the man departed, and together

Amenhotep and I walked to the edge of the boat. The sun was very near the water. It seemed as if it would disappear completely in just a moment. We dared not turn away or we would miss its departure. I did not know if this was the Shining Man, but Amenhotep seemed convinced that what I saw was what he saw. I prayed silently that the Shining Man would visit me again, although I did not pray to anyone directly or in particular.

"Now, Nefertiti. I will show you how to worship the Aten. These are sacred moves that only the initiated can offer the god. Are you ready to learn?" I remembered the greeting of Isis—the one Queen Tiye demanded I learn. I hoped this one was as simple. I nodded and he said, "Watch me."

Amenhotep stretched out his arms and raised them above his shoulders, creating an arc with his hands. Then he pushed his hands outward and bowed low toward the sun. He said, "Aten, Giver of Life, your light shines upon us all." Repeating the gestures, he invited me to follow him. We practiced, and I picked it up easily. Or so I thought.

"Almost. Turn your hands like this." Amenhotep stepped behind me and gently closed his hands around my wrists. "Up, then turn them like this." I followed his movements, out, up, and then I leaned forward, pushing my hands in front of me. His nearness felt comforting and not awkward at all.

"Let us say goodbye to the Aten now." Standing a few feet behind him and off to his right, I mimicked his steps, which he had not shown me previously. They were not difficult to master. We did this three times and then watched the Aten disappear. "Let us do this every day together, as long as the Aten rises and sets."

I smiled up at my future husband. I hoped he would always be as kind to me as he was this day.

"Tomorrow we will go to the Grand Temple and I will show you the monuments of my father."

"Very well," I said pleasantly as I watched the last of the light disappear. "I look forward to that."

"Shall we go dine?" That sounded like a wonderful idea and I told him so. My stomach sickness was long gone, and I could not wait to break my fast.

Like most meals, music played, happy people chatted and everyone hung on Pharaoh's every word. For this meal, he did not say much but we did bump hands once as we both reached for a slice of fruit. He kindly offered it to me and then sliced himself another one. I studied him as discreetly as I could. He was tall, taller than me, thankfully. His father must have been a tall man. Queen Tiye was remarkably petite. He had full lips, not feminine but well-sculpted. Amenhotep had large hands, but they were not clumsy or awkward. He was not the most handsome man I had ever seen, but he had a confidence and an inner joy that made him more attractive and interesting than most men I had known. Although I had to admit that I had little experience with men, except for Alexio.

I blushed at the thought of him. No! I swore I would not think of him. I suddenly worried that I would be forced to undergo another excruciatingly embarrassing examination. Surely not. I had heard that Egyptians did not care about those kinds of things, but the rules were often different for kings—and queens.

Leaning toward me, Amenhotep whispered in my ear, "I would very much like to kiss you right now. You are truly a beautiful woman, Nefertiti."

I wished I had worn my hair down or worn a wig because I could feel my ears warming as I blushed. I said nothing but smiled into the wine. Menmet was beside me suddenly, asking me if I needed more wine or food. I nodded and listened to the music. Most of the songs were happy tunes, often without deep meaning, but this one was different. This was about a man who waited on the shore of the river for his true love, who had sailed away on a boat. He pined for her to return, hating himself for some mistake he made. I could not help but feel sorry for him.

Sail back to me, glorious face
Return to me, my own heart
For you have taken mine with you

Without warning I thought of Alexio and how I had sent him away. How I would regret that forever! What if I had taken him with me that day, as I had intended, instead of Ayn? It was too late now, too late to go back and change things. He had taken my heart when he left—just as the song said—and I had sent him away.

I felt my lashes dampen. Amenhotep leaned close to me again, and the smell of his cedar cologne was comforting. "No more of that. Play something lively," he said to the musicians. "This is a celebration, Nefertiti. Why are you crying?"

"Forgive me, Majesty. The song reminded me of home."

"Someone you miss from home?" he asked warily. I knew better than to confess to him my heart.

"No, Majesty. The song told a story, and we are a people who loves storytelling. It may surprise you to know that I myself was a storyteller." I attempted a weak smile.

He sat up and turned to his small court. "Would you like your future queen to tell you a story?"

I should never have told him that. Now what?

As the people began to exclaim excitedly, "Yes, tell us a story!" I began to ponder what to say. Thankfully inspiration came quickly. I slid out of the chair and stood in the storyteller's position.

"Menmet, you shall help me."

"Yes, my lady," she said obediently as she took her place at my feet.

"Hear now the story of Acma, the King Who Captured the Stars."

Still smiling, Amenhotep leaned back in his chair and clapped politely, as did all who attended. I took a deep breath and began my story.

"Acma was the oldest of five brothers. His father was a good king but indecisive and sometimes weak with his counselors. As the father got older, he thought more and more about who he should choose to lead his kingdom after his departure into the next world. Naturally, his first thought was for his oldest son, Acma. Acma was tall and brave and a natural leader. Once he had killed a lion with his bare hands—a feat that greatly impressed the entire tribe. Other voices, members of the king's council, encouraged the king to consider one of his other sons. For you see, Acma had very few friends amongst the council. He was not like his father. He was not swayed by popular opinion, but he was a principled man. So in that way, he was a better man than his father. Acma was so brave and so strong that many were jealous of him. These evil counselors wanted nothing more than to see Acma lose his right to rule.

"The king's heart was torn. He believed Acma truly deserved to inherit his throne, but he felt he had to listen to his counselors. So the king concocted a competition. He would task his sons with a difficult challenge—bring a lost magical item back to the king and demonstrate how it worked. Whoever brought back the most wonderful and unusual item would immediately be made king. When the queen heard about this challenge, she pleaded with her husband, but the king was immovable on this point.

"The following day, the king called his sons to the court and issued the challenge. 'My sons, my days on this earth are limited. I hear the voices of the other world clearly, and my time here will soon end. One of you will be the next king. But as you all are so honorable, so brave, it is hard for me to decide.'

"This statement disturbed the youngest son, Axymaha, who said, 'Father! Acma should be our king. Of that there is no question. Why must there be this challenge?'

"Before the father could answer, the other sons mocked the youngest boy, declaring him a coward and unwilling to take up the challenge. The following day the brothers left to pursue their quest. The middle three sons rode in three different directions, hoping to find the elusive item that their father tasked them with. But Acma had another idea. He was not going to pursue some ancient relic in a faraway land. He knew who he must turn to for help.

"He went to Axymaha and said, 'Come, let us weave a net.' They gathered the supplies and began to weave the net.

"The counselors were amazed at this. They visited the two sons and mocked them. 'What is this? Are you going fishing? You misunderstood the challenge, Acma. This is why you will never be king. You are too stupid to rule.'

"Their words angered Axymaha, who was eager to defend his brother's honor, but Acma told him to keep his peace and continue weaving. Soon the counselors wearied of their fun and left to report to the father what his bravest son was doing. Hearing that Axymaha and Acma were disobeying his challenge, the king summoned them to question them. Surely Acma would not do such a thing! Acma obeyed his father, and he and Axymaha returned to the court, bringing the net with them.

"Just as they returned, the other sons did too. One son brought the king a gold-lined cloak that when worn would make the king young again for as long as he wore it. The king tried it on, and indeed he did appear younger. But soon the cloak grew too heavy to wear and he removed it." I waved at Menmet, and she pretended to put on a cloak. The crowd laughed at her antics. She was quite a good actress.

"The second son gave the king a vial of blue liquid. When the king drank the blue drink, he could see clearly into the Otherworld." Menmet pretended to drink an invisible drink, and her eyes grew large as she "saw" into the Otherworld. "Seeing the kings who had gone before him seated at a feasting table made him long to go there. The liquid's power soon faded, and the king could no longer see that wonderful place.

"Another son gave the king a beautiful necklace made of gold, silver and pendants of red stones." Menmet pretended to tie on a necklace and touched the stones with her hand. "The stones glowed when a lie was spoken in their presence. To test the truth of this, the king asked everyone to speak to him, one at a time. While his sons were found to be honest with their words, the counselors were not. Once the stones began to glow, the angry old king ordered the liars executed. As they were hauled away, begging shamefully for their lives, the king called Acma and his youngest son forward.

"'You see the things your brothers have brought me. What can this net do? Haven't you made it with your own hands? What magic can be in that?'"

I paused in the story here. In the Meshwesh version, Acma gives the answer, "Magic is within us," but for my future husband I decided to change that phrase.

"'Father, with every twist and loop of this rope, we prayed to the Aten,' Acma said." I heard the gathering whisper, but with one look from Pharaoh they became silent again. I continued, "'We pleaded with him to grant us our wish, and he has done so. Watch now, Father!' Together, Axymaha and Acma cast the net high into the sky." Menmet did the same, and I helped her give the illusion that we were the sons casting the net. The crowd laughed again. "So high was the toss and so magical was the net that they captured many bright stars with it. Then they carefully pulled the stars down to earth and held the net in place as their father watched in amazement.

"'This is truly wonderful, Acma! You and Axymaha have captured the stars! But why, my son? What magic is in this?'

"'You may walk upon them, Father, and they will carry you safely to the Otherworld. You see? The Aten has granted us our request.'

"'Yes, I see!' Very excited about traveling to the Otherworld now, the old king kissed his wife and hugged his sons. He stepped on the stars and stood with his hands on his hips. He said a few words of thanks to Acma and Axymaha and declared Acma king. On his command, the two sons released the net and the stars returned to the sky, taking the old king with them. From that day forward, Acma ruled as king, and his brother Axymaha served in an honorable place all his life. The net was burned as an offering to the Aten as it rose the following day. And from that day forward, everyone in Acma's kingdom worshiped the Aten, for it was he who so graciously gave them a true king.'"

I waved my thanks to Menmet, who smiled back at me and then cast her eyes to the ground. Now I could see why. Amenhotep was leaning on one arm watching me. The look in his eyes told me he was thinking intensely about my story. I remembered myself after a moment and so too cast my eyes to the ground. A hush fell over the hall as we waited for word from Pharaoh. Had I made the wrong choice? Said the wrong thing?

Then he began to clap loudly. I felt relief wash over me as the people joined their Pharaoh in applauding. He stood and called one of his servants to him. "Bring me the gift." So startled was I that I looked him full in the face without permission.

"Nefertiti, I had no idea you were such a skilled storyteller. There was much truth in the words you spoke. It is indeed the Aten that is worthy of our worship, and you do me a great honor by including the god in your story." I blushed and said nothing despite my relief. "This gift is for you. Open it now," he directed his servant. The old man eased the lid of the wooden box up, and inside was the most wonderful necklace I had ever seen. It was a falcon, its wings spread open, the wingtips held by a gold chain. Encrusted with colorful, shimmering jewels, it almost seemed alive.

I reached out to touch it. "It is beautiful, Amenhotep. Thank you."

He smiled, and deep grooves appeared on either side of his full lips. "You are truly pleased?" he asked in a deep voice.

"Beyond description. It is the most beautiful thing I have ever seen."

He removed the necklace and stepped behind me. It felt cool on my skin and heavy, much heavier than my green necklace had been. "It is fit for a queen, I think. My queen."

He stood in front of me now and surveyed me. Pleased with what he saw, he took my hand and led me around the room so the gathered guests could greet me. Without fail, each applauded loudly and said, "Well done, Queen Nefertiti." When we finished our walk we left the gathering and walked into my chambers. My servants immediately disappeared, leaving us alone. I could see that someone had scattered silky, fragrant flower petals all over my floor. I followed the path and saw where it ended. In my bed.

I looked up at Amenhotep, and he said tenderly, "There is no sense in delaying the inevitable, is there? I want to be yours, and you must be mine. Tomorrow, my priests will meet us at the Blue Stone on the way to the temple. There we will be joined in marriage, and from that day forward you will be Queen Nefertiti. Later, we will have a large wedding with many formalities. But tonight, let it be just Nefertiti and Amenhotep, children of the Aten and the Shining Man."

I swallowed nervously, suddenly wishing I had drunk more wine. "Very well, Majesty."

"No, remember. Tonight I am only Amenhotep." He leaned against a nearby cabinet. He was tall, so tall that I felt small standing next to him. He removed his crown and set it to the side, running his hands through his short hair. Following his example I released my long hair from the ebony pins that Menmet had poked in my hair.

As I reached for the necklace he said, "Let me help you." I turned and lifted my auburn curls. He removed the heavy necklace easily, and I could hear it clink as he set it next to the crown. He kissed the bare skin of my neck, and I froze as warmth filled my body. Amenhotep rubbed the arch of my neck and let his hands wander over my shoulders. I faced him and kissed him freely. His hands were in my hair, and his kisses became more urgent. Images of Alexio tried to stir in my mind, but I refused to think about him. I enjoyed the moment,

Amenhotep's fragrance and the expert touch of his hands. I could see he was no inexperienced boy but a man who knew how to please a woman.

Breaking away from his embrace for a moment, I untied the gown and stepped out of it. He watched me with an appreciative, serious smile, and we walked to the bed. He stripped his tunic off quickly, and I let my eyes drift over his athletic body. As I stood naked in the cool chamber I felt a moment of doubt. What was I doing? Then reality set in. What choice did I have? I remembered Queen Tiye's words again. Yes, I would be a queen and not a prisoner. Who was to say that this was not what the Shining Man wanted? We fell into the soft bed together; our hands were hungry for one another and our kisses increased our passion.

"Amenhotep," I said in a whisper. He shuddered slightly, so I said his name again as a small smile curved on my lips. I refused to let my mind race. I would be present in this moment. So what if I did not love him with the white-hot fervor of my first love? He was worthy of love, and I had been chosen to love him. I could not deny that I wanted him.

"Nefertiti," he said, "You are mine now. All mine."

"Yes," I said as he entered me. "I am yours."

Despite the building passion between us, Amenhotep did not hurry. He moved slowly at first, kissing my breasts and face. He was playful and patient. I got to know his body and felt as if he completely enjoyed mine. I had not expected that. It was a happy surprise.

Sometime later, we lay in the tangled sheets of my bed. His fingertips traced my face, and I kissed them.

"Do you think you will ever love me?" he asked me quietly.

"What do you mean?"

"Love is not easily produced, and sometimes it never comes. I am no fool in these matters."

"I am sure you are not, Amenhotep. I think there are seeds of love here in this very bed and in our hearts. Let us water the seeds."

He smiled, showing his beautiful teeth. His eyes were now lined with kohl, but I remembered how he looked as the gardener. Those were kind eyes, the eyes of a good man. Yes, I could love a good man. "You are very wise. From whence comes such wisdom?"

I thought of Farrah, Mina and my father. "My tribe. They are a wise people." He kissed my hand, and we looked at one another as the moonlight fell in on us from the open window.

"We are your tribe now. We are your people," he corrected me.

"I know this. Forgive me." I kissed his hand back. "I perceive that you are a good leader—one who cares about his people. For that, I am grateful."

"I have so much to do. It weighs on me sometimes," he admitted. "I am glad to have a partner in this dream of mine. A city—no, a kingdom—that serves the true god. The Aten."

"You have to know that not everyone will be happy about such an idea," I warned him.

"I know this full well. One day I will tell you about my brother; then you will know how aware I am of the price that has been paid. But no talk of kingdoms tonight. We are just two people, not kings or queens. Remember?"

Feeling bold, I slid out from under the sheet and laid my head upon his chest. I wrapped my leg around him and held him close. If this was all I had, I would make the most of it. I heard his heart beating evenly and loudly. I refused to close my eyes, for I did not want to dream about Alexio. Amenhotep caressed my arm, and soon we were kissing. After a few moments, I could feel the urgency rise in him and he was covering me again.

"What are you doing?" I said with a playful laugh.

"I am watering those seeds you were talking about."

I laughed again and kissed him wildly. Sometime close to morning, we fell asleep. I did not dream about anyone or anything. I woke feeling tired but peaceful. Amenhotep was gone, but Menmet drew my bath and prepared me for morning worship. This would be my life now. I was at peace with that. If I could help Amenhotep lead his people to peace and protect my own, so much the better. At least my life would have been worth it.

"Someone did not sleep long enough, I see. Our Pharaoh is an amorous man." As Menmet's statement was not a question, I did not feel compelled to answer.

"My hair is a mess. Perhaps today is a good day to don one of those beautiful wigs."

"Oh yes, my lady. You will look like a proper Egyptian then." She knew by my look that I was offended but quickly apologized. "Please, lady queen. I did not mean that."

"I am too tired to worry about it. Help me get ready."

"The water is hot. Enjoy the bath, and I will go find you something beautiful to wear. Is that acceptable?"

I nodded and stepped into the water, the sore parts of my body thankful for Menmet's thoughtfulness. I called to her, "Nothing that shows my breasts, Menmet." She obeyed me, and somehow at the appointed time I was ready to stand with Amenhotep to welcome the sun. This was the first time I had worn an Egyptian headdress, and I felt nervous about it. When I saw Amenhotep's face I knew I had made the right choice.

"My queen," he greeted me with a look of appreciation.

"My Pharaoh." I nodded at him, trying not to picture him as I had seen him last night. We took our places aboard the deck and, as the attendees watched, made our morning oblations to the Aten as it rose. When it was done, we disembarked with plans to make our way to the Blue Stone. I had never been, but I was anxious to see Amenhotep's kingdom—and my new kingdom.

As we stepped off the boat I saw we had a visitor waiting for us. Ramose. Immediately I thought the worst. Something was wrong at home. Zerzura had fallen. *Oh no!* Dutifully the rugged-looking general slid off his horse, wisely remembering that no one should be higher than the Pharaoh.

"General, I am surprised to see you here. What has happened?"

"Forgive me, my Pharaoh. I have disturbing news to share with you. If we could speak." He indicated that he wished to speak in private, but Amenhotep did not grant him an audience.

"You may speak before my queen, General. What has happened? Out with it." I could see Amenhotep was not a man who was accustomed to asking anyone anything twice. I warned myself to remember this. Ramose's face demonstrated his surprise at the announcement that I was now queen.

"My wife has been murdered by the queen's servant. I seek permission to pursue this girl. I believe she has gone back to her Meshwesh home."

"And you had to come out here to ask me this?" Ramose had something else to say, but he refrained when Amenhotep raised his hand. "What is this servant's name?" Amenhotep asked.

"Ayn," Ramose replied.

"Do you know anything of this?" Amenhotep asked me.

"Ayn came with me, yes, but I know of no plan to kill Inhapi. As far as I knew, Ayn and Ramose were...friendly." I added, "Ayn would not kill unless she were threatened."

"We have no time for a trial now. You may search for the girl, but if she is in Zerzura, do not pursue her. My wife will make sure she is returned in that case. I do not want to send the army of Egypt to steal back one girl. Is that all?"

Ramose wisely held his tongue. Amenhotep continued, "Then that is my command. You may retrieve the girl, but do not harm her. If she has gone home, you will wait. My wife will arrange her return when we return to Thebes."

We climbed aboard the litter prepared for us, and I watched as Ramose and his man returned to Thebes. He had not gotten the audience he wanted, and now I had the Pharaoh's ear. How could Ayn have done such a thing? Why? There would be time to discover that truth, but now was not such a time. This was my wedding day.

I felt Amenhotep's hand in mine and squeezed it. He had been correct. A crown was a heavy thing to wear. Perhaps that was why the mekhma never wore crowns. Serving our people had been a joyful thing. But now I was more than the mekhma of the Meshwesh.

I was truly the Queen of Egypt.

Epilogue

The Falcon Rises—Pah

The woman's eyes glistened as she rubbed my skin with mint oil. The cool sensation soothed my red skin, which had been burned during my trip to Thebes. My head itched still, even after the round-hipped priest had shaved my head and rid me of the ragged haircut left by the Kiffians.

Why was I here? I could not remember clearly. I took the cup of clear water that the priestess, Magg, handed me. Magg, that was her name. As I drank, I felt refreshed for a moment. It was in these moments of clarity that I remembered who I was—or at least who I had been.

And what I had done.

Now here was Magg again covering me with a comfortable, loose robe and leading me to the balcony that overlooked the center of the city. We were up high—higher than any hill I had climbed. I caught my breath as I wrapped my arms around a green painted column. The wind whipped my robe, tossing it in the air and showing my bare legs. Magg pointed and clapped and said something to me in her unintelligible, toothless language.

I looked down in the direction of her pudgy finger and saw her. A woman on her knees before a massive gold throne. Musicians were playing a frantic tune, and the people cheered the woman's name.

Nefertiti! Nefertiti!

The woman beside me repeated it, "Nefertiti! Nefertiti!" She nudged me with her arm, coaxing me to say it too.

It was my sister. I released the column and slowly walked to the edge of the balcony to get a closer look. I could not stand without feeling dizzy, so I knelt and leaned over the edge. My sister raised her hands and said some words that I did not hear. The crowd roared in response, and the man who sat before her rose, reaching out his hands to her. She slowly ascended the steps and took the seat beside him. The meaning was clear. My sister Nefret had her own crown now. She would rule as the Queen of Egypt, and I...

Why was I here? Alexio! I turned to Magg. "Where is Alexio? Where is my husband?"

"No man here. No man at all. This is the home of Isis, and you are her priestess. No man."

"I have to go home. Why am I here?"

She said something else I did not understand and waved around her. "Home of Isis. You home."

"No!" I said as I ran back into the temple and toward the dark green doors with the long golden handles. As I ran I could see the doors were closing. "No!" I screamed as I ran faster. The doors closed in silence, and I beat my fists against them until I fell to the ground in a heap.

Now I remembered how I got here. I had been walking. Walking with Astora. We were looking for the white flowers for my father's tea. He was better now but needed the flowers to get stronger. I had kissed Alexio goodbye and promised him I would return soon. The night before I had slept the entire night without any nightmares, although I did see Farrah and Paimu hovering outside my window. Sometimes I forgot my name and the names of the people around me, but he was always there. My Alexio.

See, Nefret? It is me he loves. You left, and now it is me. Just me.

Alexio, help me!

That is what I shouted when Astora led me outside. She struck me, and I fell to the ground. When I woke up, I was heaped across the back of a camel and my shoulders were burning in the sun. I screamed and screamed, but in the desert, there is no one to help you. I thought my captors were Kiffians, but I soon learned they were not. Just slavers and mercenaries. They were sent to find me, and they had.

Then I passed out. I woke up again and was staring into the eyes of the bright-eyed priestess. Who had done this? Nefret? Astora? I could not imagine, but I was tired, too tired to cry or struggle anymore. I walked back to the balcony, unafraid of any punishment the priestess might give me. She grunted at me and waved at a small table of food. I grabbed a piece of bread and shoved it in my mouth. It was stale and hard to swallow. This was not chula bread at all.

No more bread from home for me. Would I ever see home again?

The sound of her name echoed throughout the city: *Nefertiti! Nefertiti!* I looked up in the sky expecting to see a bird, and I was not disappointed. Others would not see him, but I could see his silvery outline there, just above the courtyard where my sister now sat.

Farrah had been right. The falcon would rise—and it had. Now nothing would stop it from soaring above us all.

I had been wrong. I was not the falcon.

I had always been the Bee-Eater.

Read on for an excerpt from The Kingdom of Nefertiti,
Book 3 of The Desert Queen Series

The servants lifted my heavy robes as I took my seat upon my husband's throne. The gold fabric draped over the back and across the dais smoothly under their experienced hands. I held the heavy brass crook and flail in my hands; the weight seemed easier to manage this morning. At least now the regular courtiers appeared less shocked when I sat in Amenhotep's place. He had been gone two months now—this had been his idea.

"The people need to see you as Queen of Upper and Lower Egypt. Lead them, my wife." His confidence in me gave me strength, but it did little to put my heart at ease. He was, after all, in the arms of Queen Tadukhipa even now. I had hotly contested this arrangement, but after a visit from the Hittite-Mitanni king, I could hardly stand in my husband's way. If we wanted peace with the Hittites, Amenhotep would have to honor the marriage put in place by his father. How strange these Egyptians were! Sons inheriting wives, concubines and harems. It was a strange thing indeed, but my husband assured me his heart remained with me. Like so many things in my life, this matter was out of my control. I would make the best of it. And as Queen Tiye often reminded me, the prize had not been won. Amenhotep had not yet announced to anyone who would be his Great Royal Wife; however, my rule these months was very likely a test, she whispered to me during our evening meal last night.

Another test in a life of testing, I thought wryly. I knew Queen Tiye hated Tadukhipa beyond reason, almost as much as she hated the priests of Amun. She seemed to have little love for anyone except her dead son Thutmose and, of course, Pharaoh. Poor Sitamen was ever her shadow.

Memre informed me that more royal visitors had come to the Theban court, ready to pay homage to Pharaoh. I sat up straight as Queen Tiye came to stand beside me and Huya bowed before us. With a clap of his hands, the outer doors opened and I blinked against the sunlight that poured in through the throne room. My wig itched and my stomach rumbled, but I kept my face like stone as the small contingent of foreigners approached.

From the moment he stepped into the inner court I recognized him. Alexio! With shaggy dark hair that hung about his shoulders, he wore a clean blue tunic, leather leggings and sandals. Beside him were a few others: Biel, the young man with the scarred face, had now grown even taller, my uncle Horemheb who always dressed as an Egyptian and a child. A child barely walking and with red hair!

I felt Tiye's eyes upon me, and I forced myself to breathe normally as the group approached. Alexio had not changed—he looked a little older, a little unhappier. He showed no excitement at seeing me; nor did I expect any. I had betrayed him at the highest level. I had taken an oath under the stars, swearing to love him always and call him mine. Then I sent him away.

Shaking myself out of my reverie I listened respectfully as Huya announced the leaders of the

Meshwesh. "Horemheb, friend of Egypt, brings gifts of turquoise to Pharaoh and his queen, Nefertiti. May he present them?" Dutifully, I nodded my permission, careful to keep my movements smooth and easy so as not to disturb the scented wig and crown that rested uneasily on my head. Horemheb stepped forward stiffly. He knelt on his long legs and held open a round cedar chest full of bits of turquoise jewelry. It was not a fine prize—not so fine as the gifts the Hittites and Cushites offered—but I knew it was the tribe's best. The Meshwesh were not a stingy people. I barely looked at it but thanked them for their kind gifts to Pharaoh.

"Welcome, my father's people," I said warmly. There could be only one reason why they were here—to see their mekhma and, if possible, bring her home. And I understood that although I was the mekhma who had saved them, brought them back to Zerzura, raised them to a seat of respect in Egypt, I was not the one they came to rescue.

I would never be rescued.

Read more from M.L. Bullock

The Seven Sisters Series

Seven Sisters
Moonlight Falls on Seven Sisters
Shadows Stir at Seven Sisters
The Stars that Fell
The Stars We Walked Upon

The Desert Queen Series

The Tale of Nefret
The Falcon Rises
The Kingdom of Nefertiti (forthcoming)
The Song of the Bee-Eater (forthcoming)

The Sirens Gate Series (forthcoming)

The Mermaid's Gift
The Blood Feud
The Wrath of Minerva
The Lorelei Curse
The Fortunate Star

The Southern Gothic Series

Being with Beau

To receive updates on her latest releases,
visit her website at MLBullock.com
and subscribe to her mailing list.

About the Author

Author of the best-selling *Seven Sisters* series, M.L. Bullock has been storytelling since she was a child. A student of archaeology, she loves weaving stories that feature her favorite historical characters—including Nefertiti. She currently lives on the Gulf Coast with her family but travels frequently to exotic locations around the globe.

Made in the USA
Middletown, DE
14 July 2018